"You boys wouldn't be in any kind of racket or anything?" she asked.

He glanced at her in the rear-view mirror. Daylight was not at all kind to her face.

"You know I never did find out what you boys do," she said.

"You can say we're in the banking business," Frazier said. He regretted saying it immediately. It was a comment a punk might make. You wanted to feel big so you swung it around. Just as foolish as Charlie's taking on the dim blonde in the back seat, to satisfy his uncomplicated desires. Frazier's own eyes were swimming from twelve hours' steady driving, his foot down on the accelerator.

A brown Chrysler sped by him, passing the black Ford directly ahead of him in the middle lane. The Ford was going less than the legal sixty. Frazier moved out to pass it. Ahead of him the brown Chrysler jammed on its brakes. It swerved inward, banged the black Ford and spun it out.

He heard the girl scream in his ear. The road was blocked. He could see one place to take the Olds—up over the curbing and down the center strip. He had committed himself when he saw how bad a mistake in judgment that had been. The girl's long thin scream was still piercing the air when he made his second decision and flung himself sideways toward the floor of the car, falling against the dashboard, arms clasping his head.

JOHN D. MacDONALD

CRY

HARD

CRY

FAST

A FAWCETT GOLD MEDAL BOOK

Fawcett Publications, Inc., Greenwich, Conn.

Member of American Book Publishers Council, Inc.

CRY
HARD
CRY
FAST

chapter 1

TWO hours before the accident occurred, Devlin Jamison drove over the crest of a hill on the pitted two-lane asphalt and saw, far below him, the multiple lanes of the east-west highway, the yellow octagon of the stop sign. The shocks bucked and the pale blue Cadillac convertible swayed as he went down the rough hill and came to a stop at the sign.

When the lanes were clear he turned right, heading west, accelerating smoothly. As he gained speed he began to notice an annoying thumping sound in the front end. The car had been completely checked in a reliable garage before he had started the trip. He wondered if he had knocked it out of line on the rough country road. The sound was noticeable at forty, vibrated the steering wheel at fifty and began to smooth out at sixty. At sixty-five he could no longer detect it. He checked the gauges, shifted his position slightly, drove on with the needle steady at sixty-five, handling the car with unconscious skill.

Ten minutes later a sign warned of traffic signals ahead. As he slowed down the thumping sound once again intruded itself. Beyond the light was a row of service stations, gravel blue-gray in the hot spring sunlight, buildings blazing white, pumps standing in holiday colors on concrete islands.

Jamison moved into the right lane, saw the yellow truck moving up behind him, signaled his turn and hurried it somewhat, coasting up to one of the stations. An attendant came out from the grease rack, wiping his hands on a ball of waste.

Jamison got out of his car, stretching long legs. "Is there any way you can check the alignment?"

"No, sir. We can't do it."

"The damn thing is thumping."

"There isn't anybody close by. About twelve miles west of here, on the left, is a place called Barney's Service. They've got the equipment."

Jamison thanked him and got back in the car and drove on.

Once he was up to speed he could no longer hear the thump. It could have been the rough road or maybe Gina had hit it against a curb the way she . . . .

He tightened his hands on the wheel as the grief and loss threatened to overwhelm him again. He cursed the trickery of grief. It would back off from you a little way, crouched and waiting, tail tip twitching restlessly. It would wait. It would wait until you were so far off guard that you started to think of Gina in the old way, fondly, amused at the eccentricities of her driving, aware of your love for her. It would wait for that moment and then pounce and shake you and say in your ear, "There is no more Gina. She's gone."

She's gone, and this trip is no good. This trip is a uselessness. He felt awkward, taking this trip, as though playing a part. He was taking the trip because the others wanted him to, felt it would do him good, insisted on it. Now he was going through the motions because it seemed important to them.

He knew how it would be on this morning back in the bright offices of Stock, Jamison and Vallent. Probably Joe Vallent would wander into Stanley Stock's office and say, "Well, I guess Dev got off this morning."

Stanley would be, as he was about everything, pontifical. "This will do him a great deal of good, Joseph."

And they would nod at each other in the big bright office, sane, reasonable and untouched. Jamison realized how useless it was to resent them. They were doing what they thought was best for him. To be accurate, there was a leavening of self-interest in their plan for him.

Stanley Stock had admitted it. He had said, a week ago, "Dev, the three of us have made a good team. I have the contacts, the head for business. Joe Vallent has all the steam in the world. Of the three of us you are the only creative architect. Without you we could get along. But with you, Devlin, with your sketches and imagination, we can keep on landing the juicy contracts."

Devlin remembered smiling apologetically and saying, "The wheels just don't seem to go around any more, Stanley."

"I'll be blunt with you, Dev. This whole thing has been a dreadful shock to you. You're brooding about it. You're not doing yourself or the firm any good. Joe and I have talked it over. We think you ought to pack up and go away for a while. Put your golf clubs in the car. It's May. Take off. Come back in the fall. We won't expect to hear from you. Lord knows we've got enough to keep busy on this summer. You owe it to yourself to get away, Dev. Get away from here and from the house where you lived with Gina and all the local memories. It won't hurt as much when you get back."

"Sure. Time heals all wounds," Jamison had said bitterly and when his eyes had begun to fill he had gone over to the windows, his back to Stanley Stock.

After a few moments Stanley said, "Will you do it?"

He had sighed then. "I guess I might as well. I'm not much damn good around here."

It had taken a week to get things in shape. He had dismissed the housekeeper, Mrs. Hartung, and told her he would phone her in the fall. He had arranged for a man to look after the grounds. This morning he had walked through the silent brooding rooms, looking at the things she had bought and the things she had loved. Her personal things were gone. The day after Gina's death Nancy Vallent had come in and packed up her clothing, cosmetics, costume jewelry without telling him. They were gone and he had never asked where. Nancy, full of understanding warmth and pity, had tried to take away all the too-personal things. But that cannot ever be done to a house where two people have lived in a good love.

He remembered some of the things Nancy had overlooked. The round scrawl of a half-finished grocery list on the kitchen bulletin board. A piece of green yarn she had used to tie her hair, which had gotten, somehow, into the drawer with his socks. The worst, the very worst, had been the present for his birthday. She had died the week before. He had found it in the hiding place where she always put presents. The card was with it, a comic card taunting him about his advanced age of thirty-four. He could not unwrap the gift. He took it with newspapers out to the burning barrel behind the garages and turned away as it started to burn. He smelled the stink of burning leather and knew that it had been something of leather, of very fine leather because she liked things that were very good. It had very probably been too expensive. Then he wished he had not burned it, that he had saved it as a last present from her.

Ever since her death he had found himself doing things that were almost grotesquely sentimental, or strangely cold— and regretting them immediately. It was as though he had lost the ability to act in a rational way. He had spent a whole evening remembering their worst quarrels, fixing them in time and place, remembering what had been said, remembering his own absurdities. Words cannot be taken back.

He had wondered how it would be, now, if it had been a poor marriage. Would he feel the relief of freedom? Would there be a hypocritical sadness? But it had been the best marriage. "DevandGina"—spoken as one word by their friends, because it could be sensed that they were one word, one entity. She had been joy, and she had been daring, and both those qualities—given to him by her—had shown in his work.

He could not stop his own irrational behavior, nor could he lift from his mind the heavy awareness of guilt. He knew his guilt was irrational, but it was with him. It made him wish there were something he could dedicate himself to, some great appointed task which would expiate guilt.

It had been a wet April morning and Gina was wanly wearing what she called her "rain face." She despised rain and it invariably depressed her. With her own peculiar reasoning she refused to own a raincoat or umbrella. "If I owned that stuff I'd have to go out in it, wouldn't I?"

"But you do anyway, punkin."

"Not so much."

At breakfast she had talked about a party they had to go to that evening, telling him to be sure to be home on time. She said the cleaners hadn't brought his gray suit back and she would have to go in and pick it up because this wasn't a delivery day. He said he would pick it up. She said he always forgot things like that. He said he didn't have to have it anyway. The other gray one was all right.

"But you look so darn good in the new one."

"Would you say handsome?"

She tilted her head. "Well . . . let's not get overcome here."

"Do all beautiful women marry ugly men?"

"Not ugly either. Just sort of big and rough-looking. But important. Did I ever tell you how important you look?"

"Nope."

"You always get tables in places, and good service. And people look at you and wonder about you. I think it's a kind of reserve, or dignity or something. Nobody slaps you on the back, Dev. Or nudges you in the ribs."

"Austere is the word you're hunting for."

"Austere? But I know better than that, don't I, darling?"

"Did you know that when you blush the end of your nose stays white?"

"I am *not* blushing. I am an antique married lady. Go to work, you."

"Don't bother about the suit. It's raining."

"It's no bother. You'd *never* remember it."

And so he had not protested, had not demanded that she forget about the suit. That was the burden of his guilt. But how were you ever to know?

She was in the operating room when he got to the hospital. One of the men on the ambulance had picked the suit in its paper cover out of the wet road. A wide bus tire had gone diagonally across it, tearing the paper, grinding the suit into the pavement when the wheels locked.

The fat policeman said, "I guess she just had one of those blanks people pull. The witnesses say she was hurrying, and she went out right between two parked cars and right in front of the bus."

"She didn't like the rain," Dev said.

The policeman looked at him oddly. "They got her here fast, mister. That always helps."

She was on the table over four hours. It was after seven, and dark, when they took her to a room. The surgeon had a tired face. The mask was down around his throat and he slapped rubber gloves against the palm of his hand.

"I won't kid you, Mr. Jamison. I just don't know. She's had eight pints of blood. She was pretty torn up inside. It's a case of waiting. We'll keep a close watch on her." He looked more closely at Jamison. "Better let me give you a pill."

"I'm all right."

They let him sit in the darkened room. The nurse sat on one side of the bed, fingertips on the pulse in the slack thin wrist. The night light made odd shadows. He heard a nurse laugh softly down the corridor, then rustle as she walked by the room.

He stood at the window. When he heard the sound he went to the bed. She was rolling her head weakly back and forth, saying, "Aaa. Aaa." The smell of the anesthetic was thick and acid.

He took her other hand. Her eyes opened and she looked at him with recognition and comprehension, the corners of her mouth turning up the slightest bit. Her lips moved and he had to bend close to hear her. "I'm going to . . . make it. I'm going to . . . make it, dar . . . ling."

She died a minute later. There was running, and bright lights, and the glitter of needles and sharp instructions, but she was dead. He walked out alone and found that it had stopped raining.

He drove west in the Cadillac. He thought of their childlessness. It had disturbed them. Seven years married and no children. They had been on the waiting list of one of the adoption agencies. He supposed that would be canceled now. They would have some sort of routine of removing a folder from an active file, or crossing their names off a list. Until her death he had never thought of a child as being a way of keeping alive a part of Gina. Now the loss of the child that never was seemed acute.

He drove swiftly, mechanically, maintaining a steady speed. Cars smashed by on the opposing lanes, sprinkling chrome needles in the sunlight. The road was filled with people who had never known Gina, did not know of the loss of her, would never know her.

Jamison tried to think back to the days before Gina. Before Gina this present trip would have seemed far too good to be true. A big car, with the top down and sun darkening his face. Good clothes and six months to loaf—and five thousand dollars in traveler's checks. It would have been exciting. A holiday. Because there had been poor years before Gina. He had worked for Stanley Stock. He had finished his courses under the GI Bill and gone to work for Stanley.

Gina had been the daughter of a client. That was the way he had met her. She had taken him out to see the land where the house was to be built. She had money. That had distressed him at first. He had been uncomfortable about it, even after they were married. Then he had won the two competitions. With the prize money, and a loan from Gina, he had bought into the firm. Stock and Jamison. They had done well, well enough to take in Joe Vallent, well enough so that Gina's money, even after the death of her father, did not seem so overwhelming.

They had gone out that day to look at the property, Miss Regina Lowery and Mr. Devlin Jamison. They had climbed hills, argued hotly. Finally he had said, "Look, Miss Lowery. If you are going to design this house, you need a builder not an architect. If I design it according to your instructions, you will end up with exactly what you are used to. I'll do you a house you'll learn to like, and that will be better for you because it will expand your artistic horizons."

"Don't look so fierce and indignant."

"It's my work, and I do it my own way."

"Or not at all?"

"Or not at all."

She tilted her head in a way that later grew familiar. "You mean that, don't you?"

"I mean it."

"Jamison, you are refreshing. Okay. Build us a house."

He had designed it, hovered over it while it was being built. All the while he thought of it as a house in which he could live with Gina. He knew that was absurd. But that was the way it was built. And later it became their house and they lived in it together. Now it was an empty house which stood on a hill where once they had stood toe to toe, flushed with annoyance at each other, on a day just as nice as this one, nearly eight years ago.

Forty minutes before the accident he stopped for a quick lunch. When he slowed down and the thumping began, he realized he had passed the wheel alignment place many miles back. He sat at a counter. He could see himself in a mirror. He could see the empty place on his left where she would have sat. She would have ordered a hamburg with raw onions, lots of them. She was devoted to raw onions.

Where will I go, Gina? What is going to become of me?

It was the emptiness, mostly. The lack of some great task to perform. Guilt was with him.

He ate quickly and paid and left.

Fifteen minutes later he drove through a small town named Blanchard. The super-highway went directly through the town. Two traffic lights stayed red for an arrogant length of time, imposing the authority of Blanchard on the glittering, impatient traffic. Beyond the town he speeded up again. Three lanes headed west. Traffic was heavy in both directions. He was in the middle lane. Ahead of him the lane he was on and the lane to his right were blocked by slower traffic. He slowed and watched his rear vision mirror. The highway was divided by curbing and a narrow strip of coarse grass. Fast traffic moved by him in the lane to his left. Finally there was a gap, but it was being rapidly closed by a maroon car speeding up behind him.

Jamison swung into the left lane, pushing the gas pedal down to the floor. The big car responded, the needle climbing quickly past fifty and sixty and seventy. He planned to move over into the middle lane again as soon as he could, and let the maroon car by.

His front right tire burst. The car swerved right, nearly yanking the wheel away from him. He yanked it back in time to avoid diving into the traffic in the middle lane, but he overcompensated. The front left wheel hit the raised curbing and the whole front end of the car bounced up, turning slightly in the air to come down heavily on the right wheel on the coarse grass strip, angled over toward the oncoming traffic on the eastbound lanes. Around him he heard the shrill panic chorus of tires on cement.

The front right corner of the car dipped and dug, and the back wheels hit the curbing, and the back of the car, with what seemed incredible lethargy, began to come up, the car turning, beginning the first motion of what was a long roll, lazy as a porpoise, as the big blue convertible turned in the air, in the sunshine, toward the oncoming crush of cars in the eastbound lanes.

It was one-eighteen P.M., Eastern Daylight Time, Monday, May seventeenth, six miles west of Blanchard.

chapter 2

FIVE hours before the accident occurred, Alice Scholl, standing at her kitchen stove, heard trouble start behind her at the table.

"Why don't you get your hair combed?" she heard Bert, her husband, demand of Connie. "Why don't you get fixed up? Damn it, are we going to get out of here today?"

"I can't," Connie said with fourteen-year-old indignation. "I can't yet. I can't do anything. *She's* in the bathroom."

"Alice," Bert yelled. "Alice, go on up and get Suzie to hell out of the bathroom. Right now."

Alice turned the gas off under the eggs. She did not turn and look at Bert. She knew how he would look, his face pink and bright with anger. Bert Scholl was a smallish sandy-haired man with a vivid temper. His face had not changed much with the years. It was possible to look at him and see at once how he had looked as a very young man. He had husky shoulders and long muscular arms. He was proud of his arms and shoulders and wore T-shirts whenever he could. He had been in steel plants all his life, using his muscles, and he was inordinately strong for his size.

His face had not changed, but he had changed on the inside. Frequently, of late, Alice had shocked herself by realizing that she didn't even like him any more. Long ago there had been a certain sensitivity, a tenderness even. He had tried to help her. He had become, in his home, a complete autocrat, either shrill with anger, or boisterously cheerful. His frequent use of her weary body was as quick and impatient and selfish as his anger. He had lost all the words of love. She sometimes wondered if being little had made him the way he was.

Alice left the kitchen and went up the stairs. Lately it had become easier to push down hard on her right knee as she went up the stairs. It seemed to help the dull weary pain in knee and hip. She realized she still held the greasy spatula in her right hand. She felt more tired than usual. There had

15

been a lot of work getting the house ready to leave for two weeks. And all the packing. And last night she had stayed awake until almost three waiting for Suzie to come in. Soon, though, they'd be on their way and she could just sit while Bert drove. She wished she could just stay home and let the three of them go off on this early vacation. Just sit at home and do some sewing and watch the television. That would be restful.

But Bert had it all planned. They would make three hundred miles a day, and see many points of interest and get the car covered with stickers. They would spend too much money. Bert said it was "good for the girls." The girls would snap and whine at each other and Bert would curse the traffic, the service in restaurants, the prices, the car. It was all marked out on the maps. At least she would be able to just sit.

As she reached the top of the stairs she heard the throaty gurgle as the last of the bath water ran out of the tub. The hallway floor creaked as she walked down to the bathroom door. It was open a few inches. Alice Scholl pushed it open the rest of the way and looked at Suzie, her seventeen-year-old daughter.

Suzie had gotten out of the tub and stood with one foot on the side of it drying between her toes. The small bathroom was steamy. Suzie's coarse mane of red-gold hair fell forward, obscuring her face. Alice Scholl remembered seeing a picture somewhere of a girl in that same position, only the girl wore a short frilly skirt and she was tying a shoe.

"Your father's getting mad on account of you taking all this time," Alice said.

"I heard him way up here," Suzie said, her voice sulky and sleepy. "I don't want to go anyhow."

Alice looked at her daughter with exasperation. Her daughter's naked body was the body of a stranger, a grown woman. Her skin was still golden with the afterglow of last summer's deep all-over tan. The slanting morning light in the single window emphasized the pale silky down on her body. Along the knuckles of her spine it grew more heavily. The young buttocks were round golden fruit, and the legs were long and round and slightly heavy. Alice could see one firm large breast, water droplets standing on the unblemished skin. Suzie took her foot down and put the other on the rim of the tub.

"You got in awful late last night."

"Did I?"

She had been a merry child, thin, active, laughing. But in the last two years the body had slowed and ripened, and she had become sulky, distant, difficult. There was no way to reach her. Alice had heard hints about her in the neighborhood. The girl had been out very late last night. It had been a warm evening. Alice saw the way it had been, the car blanket and the faceless man, and the ripeness of her daughter. She felt her face grow hot and she was aware of the sagging tiredness of her own used body.

Alice Scholl, with no conscious thought, took a half-step forward. She raised the spatula and whipped it against the taut buttock, using all the stringy muscles of her arm, using the springiness of the handle. The crack was like the sound of a circus whip. Suzie seemed to go right up into the air to land with her back to the window, eyes wide, both hands behind her.

"Hell!" she said in a thin high voice. "Damn it, Mom!"

"I told you to hurry."

Alice saw her daughter's shocked eyes fill with tears. She said, "I . . . I'm sorry. Your father got on my nerves. And you weren't hurrying. I . . . I didn't mean to hit you like that."

Suzie blinked her eyes rapidly. "That really *hurt!*" She turned and stood with her back to the mirror, standing on tiptoe, looking back over her right shoulder. "Hey, look at that mark!"

Alice inspected the damage. The flat end of the spatula with its pattern of holes was embossed in dead white, the holes bright red, the edge outlined in red. "It will go away," she said uncertainly.

"It stings like anything."

"You got her out of the bathroom yet?" Bert yelled up the stairs.

"She's leaving right now," Alice called back.

"What's the big rush anyhow?" Suzie asked sullenly. The bones of her face were heavy and prominent. Her mouth was wide, the lips heavy.

"You'll hurry, won't you, dear?"

Suzie sighed heavily. "Sure. I'll hurry. A big rush to go no place."

"It's your father's vacation. He's been planning on it. Let's try not to spoil it for him. And . . . I'm sorry I hit you."

"It's okay," Suzie said.

Alice went down the stairs. Connie came bounding up,

taking two stairs at a time. She was a thin child and she whined more than Suzie had at that age. Alice ate hurriedly with Suzie while Bert and Connie packed the last-minute things in the Chrysler. Alice noticed that Suzie sat down at the table a bit gingerly. Suzie wore a pale yellow sweater with the sleeves shoved up, a white skirt that fitted her slim waist snugly and flared over the heavy hips.

"You look nice, dear," she said.

Suzie smiled crookedly. "All dressed up and no place to go."

"Don't *be* like that! You can try to have a good time."

Bert blared on the horn. Alice said, helplessly, "Well, we'll just have to leave these in the sink. Check the back door again, dear. Is your bedroom window shut?"

They locked the front door and went out to the car with coats and purses. Alice got in front beside Bert and Suzie got in the back with her sister and the suitcases that wouldn't fit in the trunk.

Bert raced the motor and looked at his watch. "A half-hour late," he said.

"You said I could sit by the window, Daddy!" Connie said indignantly. "Now *she's* sitting there."

"Shut up, both of you," Bert said. He drove down the street. Alice turned around for a last look at their house. The yard would be a mess when they got back. She hoped the ants wouldn't find the dishes in the sink. She wondered if Bert had remembered to turn off the hot water heater. She decided not to ask him. They drove through the city and on out to the by-pass light. Bert kept gunning the motor while they waited for the light. When it changed the Chrysler leaped forward, tires squealing as they turned left, turned east.

Alice settled herself more comfortably in the seat. The road maps were between them. She smoothed her skirt over her knees and folded her hands. It would be nice to just sit.

Connie said, in a small voice, "I think I got to go."

Bert swore softly.

After they had stopped at the gas station Suzie let Connie sit next to the window. She thought about the cute boy at the gas station. He'd had nice shoulders. And when she'd looked right at him he'd blushed. She liked it when they blushed. The ones who blushed were nicer than the ones who didn't.

Her father mumbled something and she looked at the back

of his sandy head. His bald spot was bigger than the last time she had noticed it. It was bigger than a silver dollar. He sat hunched forward over the wheel, his chin out. He thought he was such a wonder at handling a car. He ought to take lessons from Barney.

She felt a little quiver of remembered excitement about the time Barney had run the Crescent Road light and the prowl car took off after them, red light swinging back and forth and the siren screaming at them. Barney had just put it right down to the floor. His Merc had dual carbs, shaved heads, shortened stroke and it was all relieved. He walked right away from the prowl, but he was afraid they'd radio ahead, so after he made the Mill River bend he jammed on the brakes and cut into a farm yard and turned out the lights. They sat there in the darkness and the stupid prowl roared on by. Then Barney backed out, never turning a hair, and they drove back to town at a legal speed, laughing all the way.

Barney liked driving and he talked about it a lot. He had taught her to drive the Merc. So she knew all the things her father did wrong. Like trying to fight all the other cars. The way he passed, even. Riding right on their bumper until he could swing out, and always taking chances, sometimes making the oncoming car slow right down to give him time to get back in. And if anybody wanted to pass him, he'd speed right up. He drove like it was a war all the time between him and the other drivers, cursing them and getting mad every little while.

She looked at the back of his head and it seemed incredible to her that there had been years when the high spot of her day was the time when he came home. Then she would run out to the garage and wait and he would grab her and swing her way up in the air and kiss her and carry her into the house, calling her Soupy Sue and things like that to make her laugh.

What a dopey kid! He was fine as long as you let him know every three minutes he was king of the hill, but when you had a mind of your own all he wanted to do was lean on you and tear you down. The only break in this whole thing was getting out of school for a while. It was funny to look at your own father and see what he really was. Just a pint-sized mill hand with a bad temper. And she had used to wonder if God looked like him. He had seemed so big.

Suzie looked at the gray hair of her mother's head. It certainly wasn't much of a life for her, tiptoeing around the little tyrant all the time. Maybe Mom had figured, in the beginning, that it was a big deal. So what had she gotten? Only thirty-eight years old and bags under her eyes and a figure like a sack of sand. That's what it could do to you when you figured wrong. She was lots younger than Ava Gardner and way, way younger than Lana Turner, but look at her. Just no spirit left at all any more. Except taking a whack with that spatula. Suzie clenched her left buttock and felt the soreness. It stung like a burn.

"Want to play horse?" Connie asked eagerly.

"No," Suzie said flatly.

"And I don't want no kids yelling horse in my ear," Bert said.

Connie sighed. "I'll play by myself and whisper then," she said.

"We got to really push to get as far as we figured on," Bert said.

"Don't take chances, dear," Alice said.

"I'm doing the driving."

Suzie leaned her head back and blocked out the whole world, the swaying car, the traffic sounds. This was going to mean two weeks away from Barney and she had told herself that she would use this time to decide whether to stop going with him. Yet she sensed that she had already made the decision.

In the beginning he had seemed so cool and sophisticated. He had made her feel like a dumb kid. In the beginning, when he had gotten fresh and she had stopped him, he had always laughed and that had made her feel even dumber. They were going steady and he kept telling her that she was afraid of being alive, afraid to be a woman. He would finish high school this June, and she would finish her junior year. Most of her friends went steady. And a lot of them were frank about saying that they did it. So she had said that she and Barney did it, too. She didn't want to sound like a dumb kid. They said it was all right if you were going steady.

Then after they believed that she was giving herself to Barney, it seemed pointless not to do it. But she had been afraid and she hadn't for a long time. She had done it that time of the New Year's Eve party, after the wine. It had hurt and it had scared her sober. She hadn't wanted ever to yield again. But Barney had wanted her so much and he said it didn't make any difference as long as they had done it once. So she let him. Then she had given herself to him again and it had been like going out of her mind and she had been shocked and surprised by her own eagerness.

So after that they had made love frequently. And their relationship had changed. She wasn't a dumb kid any more. In some funny way Barney had become the dumb kid. He didn't seem cool and sophisticated any more. He seemed like a little dog, begging. And she learned that she could make him do almost anything by telling him they wouldn't make love any more. She had learned that it was a power you could use.

Last night they had done it because she was going to be away for two weeks and afterward he had said they should get married. After he graduated in June he was going in with his uncle, in the wholesale grocery business. He said there wasn't any reason why she should have to finish high school. What did you learn in the last year anyway? He had it all figured out. His cousin had built an upstairs apartment and he would rent it cheap. It was pretty well furnished. Then they could live there and be married and be alone every night.

At first it had given her a flutter of excitement, the thought of having a place all her own, to fix up and so forth. But it wouldn't be all her own. It would be Barney's too. And he would be there every night. And she knew he wouldn't want to go out because it always bothered him a little to spend money. It would be more of a trap than anything, and she would have to share it with the little dog begging.

Barney didn't seem the way he had at first. Now she could sort of back away and look at him. His shoulders looked good until he took off his coat and then they kind of slumped down. He was only nineteen, but his hair was beginning to go back in one of those widow's peaks. When he was nervous his stomach got upset, and when it got upset his breath got bad, so that sometimes she had to hold her breath when he kissed her.

She wondered if it had happened like this with her mother, and if her mother had wanted to have a place of her own so much that she hadn't seen how it would be afterward. Barney was sort of cute, but he wasn't going to amount to much of anything. Not with just high school. And he was awfully jealous. He didn't like other boys to even look at her. But she knew they liked to look. She wished she wasn't so heavy in the hips and legs, but they didn't seem to mind it. At least they kept looking. A girl had to make up her mind whether she was going to get married young and be sort of trapped, or wait and do a lot with herself and get somebody who was important. You might not love him so much, but life would be nicer, and it wouldn't all be sort of down a drain before anything exciting ever happened.

Then you had to remember that Barney was religious and his religion said to have babies. She guessed she would have babies pretty often. She felt as if that was the way her body was. Babies were nice, and she felt warm when she thought of them, but they could be an awful lot of work. They could drag you down and ruin your figure in no time.

She decided she would think it over for the whole two weeks of the vacation, just to be fair to Barney, but she was certain that when she got back she would tell him that she didn't love him and didn't want to go out with him any more. He would act like a crazy man, but that couldn't be helped. There were lots of boys who wanted to take her out. Maybe some of them had the wrong idea, on account of Barney, but she would straighten them out fast. They'd find out she was no tramp.

No, sir. It would be a lot harder to be good, knowing how it was, but it was going to be worth it because somewhere, somehow, someday, there would be a man. A sort of George Hamilton type. He would be fun and sometimes he'd act like a little boy, but he could become stern. Not a temper like Daddy's. Just stern and she'd have to do what he said. He'd have a lot of money and a good education. He'd take her lots of places. He'd never get an upset stomach. He'd always . . .

"White horse!" Connie yelled. "Over there. Oh, I forgot."

"I'll play," Suzie said. "We'll both whisper. You can start with five for that one if you want."

"Okay!" Connie said, delighted.

"Keep the racket down," Bert said.

"Let them have fun, dear," Alice said.

"We got to make time," Bert said.

They stopped for lunch at a drive-in and had hamburgs and milk shakes. Bert Scholl felt better when he checked his mileage against the time. "We're doing okay," he said. "Now we're on the divided highway, we can really rack up the miles."

He ate his hamburg quickly and felt it settle into a solid lump in his middle. Meals on trips always seemed to give him indigestion. He put his glass back on the metal tray and watched Suzie walking toward the women's room, her white skirt whirling around her sturdy legs, her gold-red hair alive in the sun. She was certainly a good-looking dish. If you looked at her as if she wasn't your daughter, you felt like whistling to get her to turn around.

He wondered suddenly if any of those high school punks had tried anything with her. He clenched a heavy muscular fist. He knew he would enjoy killing anybody who tried to touch her. But they were pretty wild in the high schools these days. You couldn't tell what went on. All the kids acted sulky. They wouldn't tell you anything, or ask your advice. They looked at you as if you were some kind of dumb servant.

Before Suzie had returned he started blowing the horn for the girl to come and take the tray. He leaned on the horn in a long blast. The girl came out, insolently slow.

"You're supposed to blink your lights, mister," she said.

"Now you're finally here, just unhook the tray, sister. The money is exact. You're too slow to tip."

She showed her teeth. "My life is ruint. It would have been a whole dime, I bet."

Bert backed away angrily and swung out onto the highway recklessly, ignoring the angry blast of an oncoming truck. The truck swung around him and cut in so sharply that Bert had to apply his brakes. He put the pedal down to the floor and took off after the truck, arms tense, jaw jutted forward, pale eyes narrow. The big truck was making time. Bert got the speedometer up to eighty before the truck seemed to stop moving away.

"Please be careful!" Alice said.

"I'm driving," he growled. He swung into the far left lane. He overhauled the truck and passed it. He maintained his speed for a time to put the big truck far in the rear. He saw it dwindle as he glanced from time to time in the rear vision mirror. "Showed that joker," he said.

He took another look in the rear vision mirror. The truck was far back. They had just passed a shiny black Ford in the center lane.

When he looked at the road ahead he saw the pale blue car. Traffic in the westbound lanes to his left had been a meaningless blur. Suddenly, shockingly, a big blue convertible with the top down detached itself from the opposing traffic. It bounded high over the curb, dug its nose into the dividing strip, bounded even higher, rolling toward him, clear of the earth, suspended in dreadful slowness.

He hit the brake and tried to swing right away from it. He

rebounded from the side of the Ford. The kids in the back seat came forward. Alice had her hands braced against the dash. The blue car seemed to hang over him and he thought for a fraction of a second that he could get under it. He tramped the gas pedal down and knew as he did so that he could not get under it.

chapter 3

A half-hour before the worst multiple-car crash in the three-year history of the new hundred-mile stretch of six-lane divided highway, Kathryn Aller walked from the small restaurant along the shoulder of the highway to the service station where she had left the new Ford.

She was a tall woman, about twenty-eight, with dark blonde hair. She wore her hair in an unusual coronet braid. Her features, though delicately and beautifully cut, were somehow colorless. In contrast the thick gloss of the braid looked very alive. She wore a dark red suit, flat-heeled shoes, and carried a large gray lizard-skin purse. Though her suit was wrinkled in the back from long hours of driving, and though her driving shoes were not right with the suit, she gave an impression of cool elegance, of carefully contrived perfection. The cut of the expensive suit was flattering to her lean figure, and the hair style was exactly right for her. She gave an impression of competence, careful charm, gravity and a faint trace of severity.

"Nearly done, ma'am," the attendant said. "We'll have it down off the lift in a minute."

Kathryn thanked him and walked into the station. She took a map from the rack, opened it and found her present location. She decided that she would stop early today and plan on arriving in Philadelphia sometime around noon tomorrow. She would take a hotel room, an inexpensive one, until she could find a small furnished apartment. From then on the future was a grayness that she could not penetrate. Obviously there would have to be some kind of a job, sooner or later. Walter's generosity had made it possible for it to be later—much later. His generosity and her own savings. The word "generosity" left a sour taste in her mind. She remembered how close she had been to tearing up the check. She was glad she hadn't. It was a truly handsome check. She hadn't known how handsome until she had found it in her purse, long after that last scene.

Payment for services rendered above and beyond the call of duty. Extra bonus for the irreplaceable Miss Aller, she of the private office, keeper of the private books, secretary extraordinary.

Kathryn wished there were someone left in Philadelphia who could punish her by saying I told you so. There was no one left. Not after eight years. Eight California years which had ended in the inevitable heartbreak.

"You knew what you were doing. You knew what you could expect," Walter had said.

Yes, I knew what I was doing. Every minute. But at least, beyond all else, I was a good secretary, wasn't I, Walter Houde? The best you ever had or will ever have. A good secretary and an adequate mistress.

"You're all set, ma'am. With the gas that comes to, let me see, seven-eighty."

She gave him a ten and he made change. She went out and got into the new shiny black Ford. There were four thousand miles on it and it still had the interior smell of newness.

"Are you going to stay out here?" Walter had asked, a certain wariness in his voice.

"I'm going back to Philadelphia."

"I'll give you a letter that will get you a good job wherever you want to show it. What reason will I put in it for your quitting?"

"Family reasons. That's correct, isn't it?"

"You don't have to be nasty, Kat. Let's try to be sane about this."

"Yes, of course, Mr. Houde. Sane."

"Get your book, please."

He had leaned his big weight back in the red upholstered desk chair, turning as was his habit so he could look out of the big windows across the evening bay.

"To whom it may concern, colon, paragraph. This will introduce Miss Kathryn Aller, a secretary of outstanding competence and unusual intelligence. She was employed as a stenographer by the Eastern Sales Division Headquarters of the Allied Chemical Corporation in Philadelphia blank years ago."

"Nine," Kathryn said.

"She became my personal secretary during the first year of her employment. Later I was transferred to San Francisco to the position of Sales Manager of Allied Chemical. As I was unable to obtain a local person of equivalent competence,

I requested the transfer of Miss Aller. She has been my personal secretary ever since.

"I deeply regret her decision to return east at this time. She has youth, energy, competence and considerable executive ability. I recommend her heartily and without any reservation whatsoever."

He turned from the window then and his face twisted and he said, softly, "Hell, Kat. This is a miserable way to . . . end it."

She stood up, crisp and tall. "A copy for the file, Mr. Houde?"

"Yes, damn it."

She went out and rolled the letter head and second sheets into the electric machine and transcribed her notes in one long continuous errorless roll of the keys, ripping the paper out as she stood up. She placed them in front of him and he signed in his large bold hand.

"Kat?"

"Will that be all, Mr. Houde?"

"Good-by, Kat. And . . . good luck to you."

"Good night, sir." He was still sitting in his night-dark office, facing the bay, when she put the personal things from her desk into her purse, tilted the heavy machine down into the recesses of the secretarial desk, and let herself quietly out into the hall.

"You knew what you could expect," Walter had said.

Yes, with my eyes wide open. She drove out onto the superhighway, heading east in the fast traffic, heading back east to where it had started.

She had been terrified of Mr. Houde the day she had been asked to report to his office. His secretary had resigned. Mr. Houde had tried three other girls from the stenographic pool, rejecting each of them after a week. Mrs. Hale said to her before she left to go upstairs, "Kathryn, you are actually the most competent girl I have. I didn't send you up before because you lack self-confidence. You act like a mouse. Now put your shoulders back and go on up there and report, and look him right in the eye. He's really a nice guy, nobody to be frightened of."

The palms of her hands were wet when she stood before Walter Houde's desk. Her knees were weak. He was a big-bodied, hard-faced man in his middle thirties. It was common knowledge in the Philadelphia office that he had risen quickly in the firm, would perhaps go much higher.

"Miss Aller, eh? For heaven's sake don't jump. I don't bite. Go get a notebook." She hurried out and came back with pencils and a book, asked if she could place the book on the corner of his desk. He dictated slowly at first, gradually increasing his speed. She knew he was trying to reach a speed where she would have to ask him to repeat. It angered her. She transcribed the long letter with one minor error, writing "will" instead of "would." He took a heavy pen and put a black X across the wrong word and looked at her, waiting for a reaction.

She said nothing. He took a letter he had received, scrawled the word "No!" in the margin and handed it to her. "Write a letter to this joker. Make it formal."

She took it out to her desk, read it over, composed a reply. He read it, grunted, signed it. The whole week was like that. The week was hell. She saved her tears for the women's room. On the following Monday he called her in and asked her to sit down.

"Kathryn, I've been riding you."

"Yes, sir."

"If you have any personal opinion about it, you're free to comment."

She felt her face grow hot. "Maybe you've been trying to prove something. I don't know what. It's no pleasure working for you, Mr. Houde."

"Because it's too rough?"

"You can't make it too rough," she said evenly.

He stared at her and then he laughed loudly. "Okay, Kathryn. You're in. I live on pressure. I eat it. I look for it. I've got to have somebody who responds the same way. From now on, kid, we don't pressure each other. From now on we make a team. You don't work for Allied. You don't work for your savings account. You work for me. Can you do that?"

"I think so."

"Learn the way I think. Study the way I do things. I'll load as much responsibility on you as you can take. Don't trust anybody in this outfit but me. And I won't trust anybody but you. Your pay doubles today. And for heaven's sake don't wear yellow. It's a terrible color on you. And do something different with your hair. I don't know what. Experiment, and I'll tell you when you have it right. A deal?"

She thought it over and nodded. He stuck his big hand out. She took it. It was a strong, warm hand. She blushed. Within a few months she knew him well. Knew how so much of his irritation was the result of the continual running battle with his rich, spoiled, slovenly wife; knew how edged and relentless was his ambition; knew how rare his moments of self-doubt, of indecision; knew the chameleon dexterity with which he handled people, flattering the vulnerable, bullying the arrogant, appealing to the loyal. And knew also that there were certain basic principles on which he was inflexible—thus learning that he was much man.

She kept his appointments, administered his personal checking account, bought gifts for his wife and two children, guarded his door against the pests, the time-wasters, the opportunists. She kept his personal and his official files in perfect order, made his doctor's and dentist's appointments —all in all, she took the burden of trivia off him so that he could function more perfectly in the job he loved. As she assumed more of the burden her life outside the office shrank in proportion. She lived with an aunt who continually deplored Kathryn's lack of interest in any social life.

The best times were when the pressure of work was great and they would stay in the office late. She would go out and get sandwiches and coffee and they would work on until things were cleaned up. Then he would yawn and stretch and grin at her, maybe pat her clumsily on her slim shoulder, and go out of his way to drop her off on his way home.

When word came of his promotion it filled her with joy. He was transferred to the West Coast and all the world became dull and tasteless. It was not like the times when he had been away on extended trips. She became secretary to his successor, a Mr. Guilliam, a cold, pompous, formal little man.

The letter came to her home address two months later.

Dear Kathryn,

I have tried to make do with spooks out here, but I am weary of dandruffy girls to whom work hours are a desert between dates. I find myself burdened with the thousand and one things you used to do, and life is confusing indeed. This is a plea for help. I write you to ask your consent before I submit a request for your transfer through proper channels. Thereby I risk a few wagging tongues, but it would be for the greatest good should you agree. I can make a sturdy adjustment in wages to cover increased living expenses, and I can guarantee travel expense. If you wish to resume your life of bondage in a new setting, write me at the office and please indicate "personal" on the envelope. Local staff will indubitably try to cut your pale throat, but is that new? Please come and bring that stainless chromium roller-bearing brain with you.

Pleadingly,
Walter Houde

Her aunt was difficult. There were veiled references to "that man" and "ruining your life."

The transfer came through ten days after she mailed her response. Four days later he met her at three in the afternoon at the airport. He shook her hand warmly and said, "Lord, it's good to see you, Kathryn. Give me your baggage checks. Wait right here. The car is in front."

As they drove toward the city he said awkwardly, "This is sort of out of my line, but I knew you'd want a place to live. I really don't know the sort of thing you like, outside the office, but I guessed you'd want something easy to take care of. I looked around last Sunday and put a deposit on a place, a furnished apartment. Small, but it's got everything you need. There's a view and a private entrance. It's fifteen minutes from the office."

She felt shy. "You shouldn't have bothered, Mr. Houde."

"I guess it was a gesture. Gratitude or something. You probably won't like it. Please say so if you don't."

The street was narrow and hilly. He turned into a drive. It was a garage apartment reached by outside stairs. He carried the bags up to the small landing, set them down, took the key out of his pocket. He unlocked the door and opened it and let her go in first. He followed with the bags.

"Those big windows there make it sort of like a studio. The paneling is kind of dark, but I don't think they'd mind if you had it made lighter. The roof pitch gives you some funny angles on the ceilings, but it's well insulated. The kitchen is out here. All electric. Bath over there. That couch makes up into a bed. It looks pretty clean to me and . . . sort of cute. It's eighty-five a month but that includes utilities. All except the phone, of course. Well . . . what do you think?"

She looked at it and then she looked out the big windows. She spun around and said, "I think it's perfect, Mr. Houde. Absolutely perfect! It's exactly the sort of place I . . . I'd want to find for myself and never would."

He stood in front of her and grinned. "Lord, it's good to

see you! I've really missed you." He put his hands on her shoulders. She stood tensely, overly aware of his hands. His smile faded away and his face changed as he looked at her. He took her strongly into his arms. She stood in still fright, enduring the kiss, feeling very far from home and alone. Then something that was locked across her heart broke free and she reached her arms around the bulk of him, at first shyly, and then strongly, warmly, possessively.

He released her and went over to the windows, his back to her. She looked at the broad strength of him, and touched her fingertips to her lips wonderingly.

"We've got to forget that," he said harshly. "That kind of thing is no damn good. It spoils things. I suppose, figuring the apartment and all, you could imagine I had something like this in mind. I didn't. That's all I can say, I didn't."

"I know you didn't. I know you that well."

"We work well together. That alone is worth saving, Kathryn. This sort of act could ruin it. We've got to forget it happened."

"We can."

"I'm sorry it happened. It was my fault."

"I could have stopped it and I didn't so it's my fault too." He turned and smiled tiredly. "So we forget it. Agreed?"

"Agreed." They shook hands somewhat gingerly. He told her whom she should see about a lease, how to get to the offices, how to reach him, and told her if she needed anything to call him. He would see her in the morning. He left her alone in the new apartment. She stood for a long time at the window, then sighed and began to unpack. When she was through she explored the neighborhood, bought staples and groceries, cooked her evening meal, read for a time and went to bed. It took her a long time to get to sleep.

It was good to work with him again. But not the way it had been before. Within a month she was competent in the routines of the new position and had picked up all the odd jobs she had previously done for him. But it wasn't the way it used to be. What had happened could not be forgotten. Their response to each other had been too vivid and meaningful. The new awareness would not fade. He was too hearty and jolly, without looking at her squarely. She was too polite and smiling, and when she walked away from him, leaving his office, she sensed that he watched her and it made little awkwardnesses in the way she moved and carried herself. Physical awareness was between them like the inexorable ticking of a great clock, set for a time neither of them could guess. At busy times the sound would fade into the background, but in the silences it would grow louder and louder.

One rainy windy night, four months after she arrived in San Francisco, she was in her apartment when she heard slow fumbling steps on her outside stairs. Someone knocked heavily. She opened the door the few inches the night chain permitted. Walter stood there, light gleaming on his wet face, clothes soaked, eyes dull.

"Kathryn," he said thickly.

She let him in. She realized he was very drunk. She had never known him to drink heavily before. He stood dripping on the rug, swaying a bit. He said, "Walked. Walked all over. Hours."

He closed his eyes. She tried to support him, but all she could do was ease his fall. She could not awaken him. She wrestled the soaked topcoat off him and his suit coat. His shirt seemed reasonably dry. She put two more logs on her small fire. Gasping with the effort, she managed to drag him over to the daybed. Getting him onto it seemed at first impossible. His legs were fantastically heavy. Finally she managed it. She loosened his tie, got a blanket and put it over him. She undid his belt, covered him to the chin, went to the foot of the bed and removed his wet shoes and socks. She grasped his pants cuffs and, bracing her feet, giving one hard yank after another, managed to pull his trousers off him and out from under the blanket. She tucked his feet in, hung his clothing near the fire to dry. She sat across the small room from him and watched him while he slept. The room was full of the smell of wet wool, and the sound of his heavy breathing. She did not think of anything. She just watched over him.

It was after ten when she had covered him over. It was nearly four when he began to stir and mumble. There were a few embers in the fireplace. The room was cool.

He sat up and rubbed his hands over his face. He groaned and looked at her. "Kathryn! How the hell . . ." He groaned again and lay back.

"Would you like some coffee?"

"I can try some. I don't know if I can keep it down. I feel awful. I can remember walking in the rain. I went from bar to bar. How did I get here?"

"You walked. I let you in and then you . . . passed out."

"Brother! What a mess! I never did anything like this in my life before. What time is it?"

"Four in the morning." She went over and felt of his clothing. "Your clothes are dry, but they're pretty wrinkled."

"What a mess! Kathryn, I'm so damned ashamed of myself."

"Don't be."

"I've got to get out of here."

"It's still raining."

"I can't help that. I've got to get out of here." He sat up again, rubbing his face. She heard the rasp of his fingertips on his beard.

She looked at him sitting there and then she went quickly over and sat down on the daybed beside him. He looked at her with surprise. She pushed gently at his chest. "Lie down, Walter."

"But . . ."

"Will your wife be worried about you?"

"I don't think so. I come and go. She doesn't pay a hell of a lot of attention." He lay flat again, frowning up at her.

"You know why you came here, don't you?"

"I don't even remember coming here!"

"But you know why you had to come here, sooner or later."

After a long silence he said, "I guess so, Kathryn. But it's nonsense. It isn't any good. It's . . . cheapness. And dangerous for both of us."

"You're going to stay."

He sat up again. "No. There's no . . ."

"I know what I'm saying and I know what I'm doing, Walter."

He looked at her for a long time and closed his eyes. Her hand found his and they held hands tightly in the quiet room, much as though they were strangers who had both miraculously survived some unusual disaster.

After that beginning for them the office hours were strange. They knew the mutual danger of the furtive caress. The efficiency of both of them suffered for a time and then grew greater than before as they learned to live within this new dimension of closeness. He spent two, sometimes three evenings a week at the apartment. One drawer of the bureau became his, and one shelf of the medicine cabinet. She learned to cook the things he liked best. They did not risk going out together. He bought things for the apartment, a high fidelity music system, comfortable chairs, a dishwasher and disposal.

For over three years their physical need of each other was a continual hunger. At times in the office she would happen to catch a glimpse of the angle of his jaw, or see his broad back as he turned away, or look at his powerful hand as it rested on the edge of the desk. And then, without warning—there in the muted electrical chatter of office accounting, in that arid place of pale green routing slips, executive conferences and payroll deductions—she would feel a spreading softening warmth in her loins. Her head would grow too heavy for the slenderness of her throat, and her knees would begin a lax rebellion against supporting the ripe weight of her hips. Even the tenderest of fabrics would then chafe the tautened buds of her breasts. It showed then, in the way she looked at him and the way she stood. When he saw her in those moments, saw her with quick and eager recognition, she knew that on that night he would climb the outside stairway toward all the wanting that was there for him, waiting and throbbing.

In that first year he turned her, slowly at first, and then with a rush of momentum, into an acceptance of the flesh without shyness, without the cool reserve that had always been hers, turned her into eagerness and boldness and delight.

He was a powerful man physically, as masculine as a fist. His need was strong and rough. Sometimes on those days when, in the office, the great waves swept over her so strongly that she was afraid all could see, she would be so nearly ready for him that she could rise at once to his first quick need, sharing then an implosion that was more like combat than love, more fierce than fond.

But more often she would assuage his early need and later, on a wide plateau of passion sustained, they would, by trick and artifice, move close to the high place, and then deny themselves completion, playing this drugged game ever more dangerously until denial was overcome by their deep, compelling need.

During those first years there was ever a conflict in her— the problem of adjusting her reserved self to the great and frightening resources of sensuality he had tapped within her. Approaching any mirror she would expect to see the ravages of the life she was leading. She would expect to see a broadening and softening of lips, breasts and hips. She would ex-

pect to see in her eyes a dazed, provocative languor, see in
her very stance an exaggeration of the movements of love.

But the mirror image would be the fresh, cool vision of
Kathryn Aller, breasts still a bit bleakly virginal, hips leaner
than she cared to have them, mouth hinting of things prim.
She could not visualize that mirror image in bed, writhingly
tormented by its own devices, prim mouth torn by words
without shape or form. And so the mirror image looked out
at her and accused her.

Yet all accusations, all conflict was forgotten when his
strong hands were here and here, when muscles bunched
his back, when the sledge came down from the sky and
struck the anvil and, with spark shower, burst it asunder.

Their need was a hunger that seemed as if it could
never be satisfied, and then it was. After their first three
years physical love became more offhand, more common-
place, became merely one facet of their existence. They
often talked of the office. Sometimes they worked at the
apartment on files he would bring there.

She sensed that she was more nearly married to him than
was his wife. She cared for him—professionally, physically,
emotionally—learning all of him. It seemed that life would
go on that way. What could stop it? Though he had many
outside interests, he was her only interest. Life began when
she went into the office and opened her desk in the morning.
And began again when she heard his footsteps climbing toward the apartment he had found for her.

Then in the past year he had come to her less often,
spent less time with her when he did. He spoke half-apologeti-
cally about the many other things he had to do. She felt
that he was drifting away. She tried to hold him. She spent
a great deal more time over her appearance, shopping carefully, trying new make-up. She wanted the hours he spent
in the apartment to be perfection. Yet the drift continued.
He was absent-minded with her. And gruff. And seldom
affectionate. Their relationship in the office grew colder.

One night he came to the apartment for the first time in
three weeks and they quarreled bitterly over an unimportant
matter. He left, slamming the door. She faced then the
certain knowledge that, somehow, she had lost him. She did
not know how. She did not know where she was at fault.

The final scene occurred in the office. It was nasty and
vicious and unforgettable. She said he had become boorish,
casual, cruel, selfish. He said she seemed to have acquired

the strange idea that she owned him. He said he resented being smothered. He said she hovered over him in a most irritating way.

After the scene they both knew that it would be impossible to continue even in any form of limited relationship—as limited as a purely business relationship.

And so it ended for them.

Now, as she headed east, there was no one left to say I told you so. She had flown back five years before to attend the funeral of her aunt, dispose of her aunt's meager property.

I am twenty-eight, she thought. A competent secretary, an adequate cook, a practiced mistress. I have an air of coolness that repels people, discourages friendly advances. I have a good healthy body that will last a long time. Life is, perhaps, a third of the way finished. But everything that was to have happened has happened. All the other chapters are written. I shall inhabit an office, stiff and correct and unyieldingly efficient. In the slow wheeling of the years the memories will grow dim until at last it will seem as if all those nights belonged to someone else. Someone else held close the male flesh and made the small, soft cry of love. I shall sit sterile and erect and terrorize the young girls in the office and, behind my back, they will say the usual guessable things. I return now from whence I came, used up by the years, too dry to cry, too cold to be warmed again, assured of my own inadequacy, cleanly, solvent, clad—and quite, quite dead.

She glanced at the temperature gauge and then at the speedometer. The dealer had said to keep an eye on the speedometer. A new car might overheat. She was traveling at a steady fifty-five, five miles under the legal limit. It was the first car she had ever owned. With proper care, it would last many years. She drove in the center lane. She passed the trucks on her right and the faster traffic passed her on the left. Traffic was heavier than she had imagined it would be. She felt a great deal more confidence in her driving than when she had started out. It might be nice, once she was settled in an apartment in Philadelphia, to take a trip. During this trip she had been in tight places twice and each time her reaction time and decision had gratified her. She liked doing things well.

She heard a car coming up behind her quite fast. She looked in her side mirror and saw that it was a brown

Chrysler, going very fast indeed. She wished she could move over into the far right lane to give him a lot of room, but there were trucks in the right lane. She looked straight ahead, holding the wheel more tightly.

The Chrysler passed her. She caught a glimpse of a blond man hunched forward over the wheel, a woman beside him. When the rear bumper of the Chrysler was about sixty feet ahead of her he jammed on the brakes suddenly. The car lost speed, tires shrieking. At first she thought he planned to make a left turn. Then she saw the improbable blue car, out of context, out of reason, like a picture pasted crookedly against the scenery, the way a child might place it.

Her foot was on the brake and she had pulled even with the brown Chrysler. The Chrysler swerved into her, hard, with a clash and grating of metal, with an impact that thrust the back end of the Ford around, out of control. All the bright colors of the traffic swung by her windshield as the car spun, and she thought, sitting there, holding the wheel, that it was very like one of those Hollywood chase scenes where the camera is mounted in the fast car.

chapter 4

An hour before a huge young state trooper left the scene of the accident to be profoundly sick in the roadside ditch, Paul and Joyce Conklin, over an early lunch in the town of Blanchard, began another bitter quarrel.

As with most of their quarrels during the past two years, it began over a trivial thing. But this time the quarrel was more significant because of the environment.

Five years ago, lacking one month, they had eaten a later lunch in this same restaurant. It had been the second day of marriage, the second day of honeymoon. Joyce remembered that other meal vividly. She could even remember the face of the portly waitress who had served them, and the way Paul had made the waitress laugh. Five years ago, and she thought of it as the golden time, the time when they were favored above all other couples on earth. No other couple had been so blessed, so happy, faced such a world of promise and faith.

This was the second day of the trip which to Joyce was a trek into their past, a calculated risk, a chance to recover what had been lost. She did not know how it had been lost, or where. As with the losing of any other shining thing, it made sense to retrace old steps, looking for the glitter of it.

Joyce Conklin was twenty-six. She had a thin face, a face like that of a sensitive boy of seventeen, with its fineness and clarity of bone structure. Her hair was dark, thick of texture. Her brows were heavy, unplucked. Perhaps her outstanding quality was her look of aliveness, as obvious as the pulse that beat in her throat. Her body was thin and firm. Her gestures were quick, angular, over-emphasized. There was about her a look and aura of excitement. In rare moments of repose she seemed a plain girl. Yet in animation, in motion, in excitement she became lovely. All photographs of her were dreadful because they were static.

She elicited love because of what she was. She made friends as automatically as most people breathe because she was inevitably, deeply interested and concerned. Grocer, dentist, bus driver, meter reader—they liked seeing her and felt better that day for having seen her.

She had grown up in a home where there was love and faith and warmth and discipline. Her energy was without bounds, her optimism contagious. In five years of marriage she had given birth to two children, a boy and a girl. The first birth was dangerous and difficult because of her narrow pelvic structure. The second child, the boy, had been delivered by Caesarian section.

The last two years had marked her. Gestures which had been expansive were now merely nervous. Dark shadows under her eyes gave her a more delicate look. She was more often grave and quiet.

Paul Conklin was a far more complicated human being than Joyce, his wife. He was twenty-eight, dark, lean, two inches taller than she. His childhood had been served, as a sentence is served, in that emotional wasteland of a home which should have been broken and was not—a home where hate is a voice beyond a closed door, where contempt is a long intercepted look, where violence is a palpable thing in the silent rooms.

After reaching in every direction for security he had reached within himself and found it in the exercise of a brilliant though erratic mind. Only through intellectual arrogance could his mind—that place of safety—be made known to others.

At fifteen, after two blinded years of absorption and study, with all the world shut out, he defeated the almost-great in the chess world. The truly great defeated him because he lacked the patience to accept the discipline of the static game against equals. A year later he gave it up. When he was eighteen small experimental groups were playing his music. It was brilliant music, atonal, polychromatic, edged and daring. Yet to hear it was like handling shards of ice. It told of nothing but its own brilliancy.

At twenty he published an antisyllogistic approach to symbolic logic which created a flurry in the field of mathematics. At twenty-two, after eight months of psychoanalysis, he joined a Trappist Monastery. He fled after two months and found employment in the actuarial department of a major insurance company.

Wherever he had gone, he had taken arrogance with him. In any group he was a silent face on the fringe, reflecting contemptuous amusement. Either that, or the group was an obedient frame for his own unequivocal pronouncements. Thin, bitter, brilliant, acid, contemptuous. And as lonely as the last man left on earth.

At the insurance company he was used and knew it. He worked alone, and did valuable work. He was translating experience data into forms which could be used by electronic computing equipment to give a more detailed and flexible analysis of rate structure than any method hitherto used. It was creative mathematics, uncomplicated by human factors. It was merely a multidimensional expansion of the chess board on which a thirteen-year-old had once, with awe and excitement, learned the moves of the pieces.

Joyce MacAllen was the new girl who brought data up to him from the floor below. He flicked her with the corrosive edge of his mind. She laughed, and was warmly, personally curious as to why he should be so strange. He thought it was some sort of defensive gambit on her part. And then realized that her warmth was genuine, her interest genuine. She was fire and comfort and he came forth, reluctantly at first, from the blue icy caverns of his mind and found himself warmed, and then loved. He had not been loved before. Something came cautiously to life inside him, wary of the expected rebuff.

They were married. He told her it was a pagan rite, with a masochistic ceremony, but he smiled when he said it. He approached her mind and her body with awe carefully concealed. He was a savage who finds and worships the fire goddess. He had believed only in the intricacy of the convolutions of his own mortal brain. Now he came to believe in her, and she was destructive of his own nihilism. For three years Paul Conklin, warmed by her spirit, was a whole man.

Two years ago it had started to come back. All of it. The black moodiness. The compulsion toward rejection. The walls of ice. Step by step he had moved back from her into the inner comfortless caves so that her warmth had diminished to a pale seldom light against his face. He knew what he did. He saw what it was doing to her. He loved her. He could not help himself. He could look upon himself with objectivity and see the withdrawal and try to halt it and know that there was no lever, no brace, no handle.

This quarrel was like too many others. Because of the new highway it had been difficult to locate the restaurant.

The look of the town had changed. Joyce had been uncertain at first, but quite sure as soon as they had walked in.

They took a table for two by a side window. She smiled across the table at him. "Even the same table, Paul."

"I'm not that clear about it."

She refused to be depressed by the flatness of his tone. "I'm sure it's the same one," she said.

He unfolded his napkin. "Just think," he said, "this might even be the same spoon, dear."

"Paul, don't say it like that."

"How should I say it? I'm accepting your fetish. I'm carrying it just as far as I can. Wouldn't you like it to be the same spoon?"

"You call it my fetish, but you agreed that we should try it too."

"Certainly. I'm willing to take a trip. But you're the one who wants all the same ritual all over again. As much of it as you can get. If we do all the same things, it's like saying abracadabra. It's mathematically possible that this is the same spoon. They must last five years or better. This spoon looks at least five years old. Of course there is the normal process of attrition. People carry them away. They get thrown out with the garbage. But so long as we are emphasizing similarities, this could be the same spoon. To find the mathematical probability of this being also the same fork, you have to multiply the total number of spoons by the total number of forks to give you—"

"Stop, Paul," she whispered.

The waitress took their order. When she went away Paul said, "It's a simple formula. Suppose they had three hundred each of knives, forks and spoons. The odds of picking the same spoon would be three hundred to one. To pick the same spoon and fork would be ninety thousand to one. And the odds would be two million seven hundred thousand to one against getting the same set of three."

She looked down at her hands in her lap and felt the slow burn of tears in her eyes. "You make it silly," she said.

"I'm just going along with our program."

"You try to make it all silly."

"I'm trying to keep a balance. I'm not a mystic."

"I just wanted to come here because . . . it's the same place."

"And things were dandy five years ago in here so you can walk in and find them just like they were."

"You can't find anything you don't look for, Paul."

"But don't you feel there's something sickly about it? A kind of plaintive sentimentality? I keep listening for the sound track. Wouldn't they give us violins for this sequence?"

"They wouldn't film this, the way it's happening."

"No, I guess they wouldn't. Though maybe they would, come to think of it. You know. Stiff and alien with each other, all that sort of thing. Then comes the moment of realization, when eyes glow and the violins get louder."

"Paul!"

The food was brought to them. She glanced at him as she ate. He looked far away as he ate with methodical neatness. She looked at him and wondered what had happened to them both. Five years ago this room had been a magic place. But the words and the years had turned it into a drab room filled with the sound of traffic. The food was tasteless and somebody was quarreling in the kitchen.

She told herself she was not such a fool as to expect that marriage would continue to be the breathless experience it was in the beginning. Yet a good deal more than this should be left—a good deal more than two people who used their special knowledge of each other to inflict pain. Paul seemed to have grown back into the arrogant cruelty of adolescence. She sensed his resentment of home and children and marriage. She felt that he abused her because she was the symbol of unwilling bondage.

Paul Conklin sugared his coffee and stirred it slowly. He kept his face still. He had shamed himself in spoiling even this small thing for her. But the code would not permit the expression of shame or regret. He was aware of his own compulsion.

He could look coldly back on the history of compulsion. He remembered the very first time, long ago in the dark quiet house. He had been small. There had been a quarrel, one of the worst ones. Then they had bought the train for him. A shining and fabulous train. They had set it up in a spare room. He could remember the smell of it, the spicy electrical smell. There was a station with a light inside. There was a yellow car that carried logs and dumped them when the right switch on the transformer was pulled. For the hour that it ran around and around the tracks, he had loved the train.

He took the bright cars, one by one, and put them half in and half out of the closet, next to the door frame. He jammed the heavy closet door against them, one by one. The engine had been last and most difficult. When the cars were all spoiled he had stepped on the tin station until the light went out. They shook him, hurting his arms, and took the train away. He didn't see it again.

He remembered the strange little man who had treated him, years later, a little man with so many nervous tics and habits that he seemed mildly mad. "I can try to tell you in simple terms, Mr. Conklin. I will tell you but you will not really hear what I say. When you badly needed love you were without love. So always you have punished yourself, blaming yourself because of not being loved. The train is such an instance. And the chess that you told me about. And the music. You cannot accept any gratification without looking about for a means of destruction. It is a negativism in you. And I tell you this, sincerely, importantly. You may one day think of destroying yourself. When you think of that, stop and ask yourself why you punish yourself."

You were a serious man, Doctor. You looked at my mental tests and you were sad about me because I represented the waste of so many things. But you were wrong, Doctor. You thought love, if I would accept it and try to give it, would cure me. It did, for a time, but it was not permanent.

Now I have Joyce. And she is the shiny train, and the bold two-bishop attack, and that duet for cello and clarinet. All the bright loved things and more than any or all of them. Inside myself I cry and reach out for her, but I show her the cold grin, and I make silly nonsense out of the things of her heart, and slowly, certainly, I drive her away. It is taking a long time because she is in love and stubborn. But I can kill anything, Doctor. Anything in the world. I was born with that wild talent, and I am very good at it. I will drive her away, kill her love. She needs a warm safe man in her house, to give stability and affection to her children. I belong in the cold places. I feel as if each day I say good-by to her a thousand times.

"Do you remember how you made the waitress laugh?" Joyce asked uncertainly, shyly.

He remembered. But the perverse demon kept him from admitting it. "Don't tell me I tickled her. I can remember quite a few lapses of dignity, but nothing quite that basic."

"No, it was something you said about the . . . well, never mind, it wouldn't sound the least bit funny now."

"Go ahead. Tell me."

"I don't want to now, Paul. You'll just make some sort of crack about it. And you don't really want to know."

"I guess I should remember. I could try it on the sulky damosel we have this time. Maybe we'd all roll on the floor together, gasping."

"Are you through?" she asked quietly. "Signal for the check. I'll be back in a minute."

He watched her go through the doorway toward the rest rooms. She carried herself carefully lately, as though she had become brittle. He paid the check and tipped the girl. He was standing by the door when Joyce came out. She gave him a smile he recognized. Somehow, incredibly, she had regained her resiliency. The bitter conversation was not only forgiven, it was actually forgotten. Her insane optimism seemed to him, in that moment, to be a terrifying thing. It was not believable that she was able to continue hoping that this trip would turn out right for them, mending all the rents and abrasions.

They walked across the parking lot to the maroon Plymouth. He unlocked the car and they got in.

"It's better weather than it was that day. Remember, we ran into rain in the afternoon," she said.

"Ah, yes. A romantic rain that continued on into the night, going pitter-patter on the motel roof while we lay locked in each other's arms. Shouldn't we try to whistle up a storm?"

"Do you have to be smart about that too?"

"Am I being smart? I thought I was being pretty good. I remembered the rain, didn't I?"

"I don't know what it is . . . whatever I say you make it sound as if five years ago it was all a lot of nonsense. But it wasn't. You can't make it nonsense by talking that way about it. I won't let you spoil anything for us."

He drove out into the westbound traffic. "Things should be in perspective," he said.

"*Your* perspective. That's where you want things lately, Paul. All cut down and the shine rubbed off. So that everything is just . . . ordinary."

"Everything is pretty ordinary, dear, when you take a careful look at it."

"Like love?"

"Now I don't believe that even you would say that love is exactly an unusual state of affairs. It's a pretty well-established reflex."

"Reflex!"

"Of course. Continuation of the race. All that sort of thing."

"I suppose you've given up believing in that too?"

"Now I have to watch myself, or you'll throw the clincher at me. You'll tell me I don't believe in babies. But before you go that far, darling, take a good steady look at the race too. Can't you see some arguments in favor of discontinuing it?"

"I shouldn't be serious because you're not being serious. But you asked me. No, I see no reason to discontinue it. People are good. There's good in the world. I believe in that."

He was picking up speed west of town. The lane on the left was clear. He smiled ahead at the empty road. "Incorrigible optimist," he said. "People stink. Accept that and you have a starting place."

She did not answer. Ahead of him a blue Cadillac convertible pulled out of the center lane to pass. Paul Conklin did not reduce speed. As they passed the car in the middle lane he saw the blue car swerve right. It swung back and hit the curbing and bounced up into the center strip, but the blue tail of the car was still in his way. It was moving out of the way, but not quickly enough. He could not brake and move to the right because of the car he had just passed. The world and space and time seemed to be moving with a painful slowness. He pushed the pedal to the floor knowing that his only forlorn chance was to ease quickly through the space between the fins of the big Cad and the car on his right.

chapter 5

FORTY minutes before her violent death the girl on the back seat woke up. Frazier, who had been behind the wheel of the green Oldsmobile since midnight, saw a section of her face in the rear vision mirror when she sat up.

"I feel sick," she announced in a puffy voice.

"You should," Frazier said.

"Where's Charlie?" she demanded plaintively.

"He's right here, sleeping it up."

She leaned forward and looked down over the back of the seat. Charlie slept with his head against the arm rest. "Oh," she said, and leaned back. "Gee, I feel terrible. Where are we?"

"We'll be in New York tonight some time, Lou."

"You must a flew. Say, I forgot your name."

"Jim."

"Oh, sure. It was a pretty busy evening, I guess."

"It sure was."

When he glanced at her in the mirror again she had taken a small nylon brush out of her handbag and was brushing her young blonde hair. Daylight was not at all kind to her face. She wore a white satin off-the-shoulder blouse.

"I guess maybe this was a kind of crazy type thing," she said.

"You and Charlie thought it was a dandy idea last night."

"Sure, I know. But you know, drinking and all. You get all kinds of ideas when you get drinking. Big deal. Big thing. Honest, I just got what I've got on and that's all and let me see here, seven, eight, twelve. Twelve bucks. Are you boys going to make sure I get back down there?"

"That's Charlie's problem. You're his guest."

"Wake him up, will you?"

"I'll wake him up when it's time for him to drive."

"I got a terrible taste. Could we stop some place maybe?"

"Pretty soon."

When he glanced at her again she was biting carefully at

46

a Kleenex. She took it away and examined her freshly painted lips.

"I look better maybe, but gee, I feel terrible. You don't sleep good in a back seat. My legs kept getting pins and needles. This was a crazy idea, believe me."

"You're only young once," Frazier said.

"Sure. I guess so. Honest, I feel old as the hills this minute. Is there a drink or anything?"

"Look around back there. Maybe it slid under the seat. There should be some left."

After a few moments she said, "Got it. You want any? There isn't much left."

"No. Go ahead."

After a while she said, in a huskier voice, "That's going to help. It's nasty warm like this, but you just got to take it like medicine, I guess. Honest, I didn't even tell my girl friend. She'll think a maniac got me or something."

Frazier felt a wary tension in his middle. He kept his voice casual. "Would she be likely to call the police?"

"Francie? Hell, no. We figure, Francie and me, that we each got to live our own life. If I take off, she waits until I come back. You know, we were having so much fun in that joint last night after you two came in and Charlie started talking to me that I never did find out what you boys do."

"We've been on a vacation."

"I remember you got Florida plates on the car. Is that where you're from?"

"You can say we're from all over, Lou."

"I guess you're the type doesn't tell people much."

"Well, you know how it is. A little vacation and you don't like to talk about business."

"Sure," she said unconvincingly. "I feel a little better. If you don't want any, I'll finish this off."

"Go ahead."

After a few minutes she said, "You boys wouldn't be in any kind of racket or anything?"

"You've got a lot of crazy ideas, Lou."

"I just wondered. It would be all right with me. I mean I wouldn't sweat any. You both sort of look like maybe you could be. Oh, not rough or anything. It's just a look. Like I said, it wouldn't matter. I know the score. I was waiting for a boy for a long time. He kept saying the parole would come along just about any minute and I ought to be patient and so on. But he's still in. A girl can't wait around forever. I didn't mean to be bossy, asking like I did."

"You can say we're in the banking business," Frazier said. He regretted saying it immediately. It was a comment a punk might make. You wanted to feel big so you swung it around. In its own way it was just as foolish as the load Charlie took on last night. Load and dim blonde.

It had been Charlie's turn at the wheel, and they had been pushing it. He had sensed the irritability and restlessness in Charlie, and knew it would have to find an outlet soon. Charlie was fine when he was at the point of action. Cool, quick and smart. But he couldn't hang onto that state of mind during a long run. It was nine o'clock and dark and Charlie kept inching the speedometer up over the legal limit. Each time Frazier would comment on it, Charlie would snarl, but he would drop it back. It would be a poor time and a poor place to be picked up.

They went north along a long straight stretch, swamps on either side, wooden boards rumbling on the bridges. Frazier saw town lights ahead against the sky. Ahead, on the right, he saw a brightly lighted roadside joint. It was a square building on piles, local jalopies flanked in front of the place. The neon was pink and sick green, reflecting on the beards of Spanish moss that hung from the near-by oaks. Charlie braked sharply and turned into the rutted parking area.

"This is no good," Frazier said.

"The hell with that. I got to have a drink. What can happen here?"

"These places get checked."

"So they get checked. Come on. You can drive from here on."

They locked the car and walked to the place. The juke was loud. They walked through the sticky night and up the steps and into the place. There were about thirty or forty people there and they all looked at the newcomers. Frazier didn't like the setup. These were locals. They were outsiders. If Charlie saw a woman he liked, there could be trouble. There were women at the long bar, and women in the booths. Some of their men were in sport shirts and slacks. Others were still in their work clothes. The women looked uniformly cheap, loud and drunk, the kind of women Charlie liked. Frazier preferred a different type. Quiet, clean ones, in good hotels, in good restaurants.

They found a slot at the bar and Charlie started drinking straight shots. Frazier kept on beer, to Charlie's disgust. When Charlie left him without a word, Frazier braced himself for trouble. The two girls were in a booth. Charlie took his drink over and sat down next to the blonde in the white off-the-shoulder blouse. She was as good as anyone could find in the place. Her partner was small, round and dark. Frazier waited for two of the men to go over and try to move Charlie out. Charlie beckoned to him. He went over slowly and sat down with his beer.

"This here is Lou and that there is Jeanie. This is Jim, girls."

The blonde was pretty lush, but the dark one was a loud nothing. Frazier tried to relax, but he couldn't stop worrying. They were wasting a lot of time. Charlie knocked the shots down and his eyes got that strange bright look. Charlie danced with the blonde quite a few times. Frazier danced once with the dark-headed one. He kept trying to signal to Charlie that they should be on their way, but he didn't get anywhere. The one named Jeanie found a happier friend to dance with.

Frazier went back to the bar, nursing beer. He kept checking on Charlie and the girl. The second time Frazier came out of the men's room, he couldn't see Charlie or the blonde. It was nearly midnight. He looked the whole place over. He went on out to the car. Charlie and the blonde were in the back seat. He heard her laugh when he walked up to the car.

"Hey," Charlie said. "Get in and let's get rolling. Where you been?"

"Kiss her good-by then."

"Hell, no! Lou is coming right along, aren't you, darlin'?"

"Going on a trip," the girl said solemnly, and then laughed again.

"Look, Charlie. Wait a minute."

"Get—behind—the—wheel—and—drive," Charlie said in an entirely different voice. Frazier knew he could do nothing with him. Maybe it wouldn't be too bad.

"Go get Jeanie," the blonde said. "She'll come too."

Frazier ignored her. He got behind the wheel, started the car and headed north. The blonde complained for a while and then quieted down. He drove through the town and on into the night.

A faster car came up behind them when they were five miles beyond the town. Frazier tightened up and looked in the rear vision mirror, looking for the gleam of red spotlight. But it was a civilian car. Before it swung out to pass them, Frazier, looking in the rear vision mirror, saw that the rear window of the car was bisected by the blonde's slim leg. For a time he was annoyed at Charlie, jealous of Charlie's blissfully uncomplicated desires, his complete lack of fastidiousness. The blonde cried out shrilly once, and that was all.

Frazier drove on through the night. Some time later Charlie clambered over into the front seat, grumbled and muttered and settled himself down to sleep. Frazier kept the needle steady on the speed limit. The warm night swirled by the big car. They headed steadily north.

Now he felt the ache of twelve hours and more of steady driving.

"Can I climb over in front and sit between you?" the blonde asked.

"No."

He wondered if he should pull over, give her some cash and let her out. Charlie might be glad to wake up sober and find her gone. But he might not. Frazier wished he'd demanded the split earlier. Then he'd have only himself to worry about. His half was back there in the luggage compartment, packed inside the extra spare. Round and firm and fully packed. And time for his draw.

In spite of the dim blondes and the current item, Charlie was as good as you could find. All timed down to the last piece of a second. No pain, no strain. Walk in and walk out and drive away.

"When are you going to stop?"

"Pretty soon now. Then you and Charlie can sit up front here and I can get some sleep in the back."

He knew he needed sleep. His face felt granular. Every once in a while his eyes would swim and he'd have to shake his head. Twelve hours' steady driving was about as much as a man could take.

"You boys should have brought Jean along too. She wanted to come. Then there'd be more company."

"I didn't like Jean."

"Everybody likes her. She's an awful lot of fun when you get her going. We went there to Red's together last night. I think she was kind of sore when I left with you two. She's almost my best girl friend. I'd feel better about all this if Jean was along."

"We can't go back and get her."

"You don't have to be nasty. I was just saying that."

"You say a hell of a lot. Shut up for a while."

"I didn't know it was going to be like this," she said distantly.

After she lapsed into silence her words kept echoing in his mind. I didn't know it was going to be like this. Well, neither did I, lady. I didn't know anything was going to be like this. Neither did proud parents beaming down into the crib of one James Hallowell Frazier thirty years ago.

He wished he could have Charlie's eternal confidence. But even confidence wasn't enough when you knew that the files were being collected. Random bits of description, carefully gathered. One fine day the boom would be lowered again. They'd welcome you back into the Big Yard.

And they'd sing the same sad song. "Frazier, I fail to see why a man of your education and background and war record turns to crime."

Explain it to me, Doc. I'd like to know too. How can I be so stupid? Just think, I could work for forty years and if I saved ten dollars a week, I'd end up with over twenty thousand bucks all my own. That's a lot better way than picking it up in one afternoon.

"You don't spend money lavishly, Frazier, when you have it. The mere act of acquiring it seems to answer some need in you."

Could that be, Doc? Do you think a fellow would get so he'd look forward to those minutes just before it happens, to the sweat and tension, and everything honed keen and fine and close? Right up on the thin, hot tip of one minute of being alive? Could that get to be a thing with him?

"You were not a disciplinary problem before. I assume you will react in the same way."

Work all day and dream all night, Doc. Remembering all the scores and thinking of the big one to come, the big, fat, ultimate, incredible score where they have to write it in seven figures.

"In one sense I suppose you could be considered a psychopath, Frazier."

Me, Doc? Psycho? Unless you say Willie S. is one too. They asked him why he robbed banks and he looked at them rather blankly and said because that's where the money is.

My friend Charlie might be a psycho, Doc. He hasn't killed anybody yet, but he thinks about it. He wonders how it would feel. I know how it feels, Doc. But I did it legally, in full accordance with the table of organization and equipment, with my name inscribed on the morning report, squeezing them off like I learned on the range down at Fort Bragg, N.C.

We're just chasing the big score, Doc. But if we caught it, it wouldn't be quite big enough. Now you take any little managerial cuss living in Levittown. Isn't he chasing a score too, along with the eventual ulcer? He probably has his hot flashes when there's an opening upstairs.

"Are you going to buy me something to drink?" the girl asked.

"Honey, you like to punish yourself."

"Won't this thing go any faster?"

"Lots faster, but we obey all the little signs."

"Is it a hot car?"

"Hot, Lou? I'm comfortable. How are you?"

"You know what I mean. Why don't you wake Charlie up now?"

"Lou, dearest, up ahead someplace is a wide place in the road called Blanchard. It has a bean wagon made of shiny aluminum. We shall stop there and eat and from then on old Charlie will drive."

"He isn't as old ~~ ~~u are!"

"He is a lot younger in one sense and much older in another."

"You talk funny. You talk sometimes like the television."

"Get your paw off the back of my neck, child. Charlie is your boy."

"You're both cute."

"Extremely."

"Do you think Charlie will let me stay for a while? Last night he said we'd have a lot of fun."

"You'll have to discuss that with him."

"I never did anything like this before, going off with a boy I hardly know at all. You shouldn't think I go around doing stuff like this. I was bored. You know how it gets. Same old stuff. Same old people at Red's. Then you two came in."

"We walked right out of a dream."

"Huh? Well, you say it funny. I mean we had fun after you boys got there. I wisht we'd brought Jeanie. She'd knock you out, honest. She'd do anything for a laugh. She was even with the circus one year. Honest. There was this guy and she had to wear practically nothing and hand him clubs and balls and chairs. He juggled. He beat hell out of her once too many times, though, and she quit right there and got a job in Red's. That's how I met her. Is there another bottle maybe in the glove thing?"

"No."

"How'd you get that scar on the back of your hand any-how? You know, you've got strong-looking hands. I like a man with strong hands."

"Don't forget Charlie."

"All he does is sleep. Jim, I want you should take me shopping when we get there. I got to have other clothes. And I like to know what a man likes. That's the best way to buy your stuff, with a man telling you what looks yum."

"Yum?"

"Sure. You know. Like you wanted to look twice. Where is this Blanchard anyhow? I got to go something terrible, excuse the expression."

"Just up the road."

"I bet you wouldn't guess it, but I damn near got to be Miss Tennessee the year before last."

"No!"

"You don't have to say it like that, mister. I'm not kidding you. I got a good build. Thirty-four, twenty-four, thirty-four, and I can do talent things like sing and dance and do monologues. Anyway, the girl that got it, you could tell it was all political."

"Did you get a consolation prize?"

"You know you ask stuff with a nasty sound in your voice. You needn't think I'm some kind of tramp or something. Just because I came along with you boys when Charlie was being fun and asking me, and it was all kind of a joke. It was just one of those drunk things. I even wish I hadn't come."

"You are not alone, dear."

She was sitting on the edge of the back seat, her arms on the edge of the front seat, chin on her wrist, left elbow pressed warmly against his shoulder. She smelled a bit stale. He felt oddly sorry for her, sorry for this fiasco of what had seemed to her like a bright gay trip.

"Where did you come from originally, Lou?"

"Me? Oh, I was born in a place called Farrel. That's near Sharon, Pennsylvania. But we left there when I was real little." She sighed dramatically. "I guess I've lived a lot of places since then. I guess you could say I've had a tragical life. I had a little girl once. She died after two weeks. She had water on the brain. I was married then. I still am, because he just took off, but I make like I'm not. Gee, why am I telling you all this stuff."

A brown Chrysler sped by him, passing the black Ford directly ahead of him in the middle lane. The Ford was going less than the legal sixty. Frazier moved out to pass it. Ahead of him the brown Chrysler jammed on its brakes. It swerved inward, banged the black Ford and spun it out.

He heard the girl scream in his ear. The road was blocked. He could see one place to take the Olds—up over the curbing and down the center strip. He had committed himself when he saw how bad a mistake in judgment that had been. The girl's thin long scream was still piercing the air when he made his second decision and flung himself sideways toward the floor of the car, falling between the dashboard and Charlie's knees, arms clasping his head.

chapter 6

TEN minutes before the sleek fast traffic of Route 56, six miles west of Blanchard, was transformed into shrieking, spinning, grinding chaos, Stanley Cherrik measured the mileage against the implacable clock in his mind. He had a comfortable margin over his schedule. Westbound on the Cleveland-Wilmington run, Blanchard was a check point for time. He should go through it no later than one-thirty. Today it would be a little after one-fifteen.

The big rig was rolling smoothly, fourteen good treads against the pavement. The air lines were holding good pressure. The new picture of Buddy, the youngest, was Scotch-taped to the dash. He took a quick glance at it for luck. A very quick glance. Cherrik never took his eyes from the road for more than the smallest part of a second.

It made him feel proud of himself and amused at himself to think of Buddy. There had been three kids, the youngest fourteen, the oldest in the Army, and then Buddy had come along. Pretty damn good for an old man. Not so old, though. Forty-two. Ruth was forty-one. It was harder for her, having a baby. She'd been gloomy about it at first. But now that Buddy had come she felt a lot better about it. And the other two kids helped a lot taking care of Buddy.

Cherrik was a small wiry man with a round hard belly, powerful clever hands, a lined cheerful face and hair like steel wool. He was popular with the dispatchers and the other drivers. He'd gone with Quin-State back when it was called Harbor Transit Lines and ran only ten trucks. That was twenty-one years ago. Now they had over five hundred trucks and Cherrik was senior driver, holder of two company gold medals each for ten-year stretches of accident-free driving, plus of course the National Safety Council awards.

Each year Marsh would say, "Time you came inside, old man. Time you got off those wheels before somebody gets killed."

"One more year, I think. One more year. I hate it so bad I can't stop."

"You've pounded your brains out on the road, old man."

Now, he thought, this is the last year. Too many years of riding them when they all had square wheels. Not like now with the springs and cushions and everything.

For the last two years he had worn a webbed support like a girdle. It had eased the pain in his kidneys. Ruth had kidded him about his girdle. It had bothered him a little to be kidded. He'd never known exactly how to take kidding. He guessed he took too many things too seriously.

Like driving a truck, for instance. Take the smart kids. They make out like it's a job for morons, maybe. Sit and turn a wheel. Wear the company monkey suit. He hadn't liked wearing a uniform at first. Then he learned how it began to mean something. You had a job. You dressed for it. Other lines could have drivers who looked like bums. But on Quin-State you knew you were good. You had to be or you wouldn't stay there.

The old man, Marsh's father, had said it once before he died. "Cherrik, I am not going to put twenty thousand dollars' worth of vehicle and forty thousand dollars' worth of cargo into the hands of some wild man and then trust in God and the insurance company to take care of me. We can bid low rates and pay top salaries because we hire and we keep men like you who want to do things right. Have to do them right. Mine is a public responsibility. I can't afford to put killers on the road. Killers are men who take chances. Some of the drivers get sore because I hire men to spy on them on the road. You watch the ones who complain. They're the tailgaters. They're the boys who let the terminals do all the checking on maintenance. Anybody asks you what you do for a living, Cherrik, stick your chin out and say you drive a truck."

Even after all these years, he still got a boot out of it. Hammering the hills in the first light of day, shifting at the precise moment, racking up the miles, pulling in for coffee where dawn paled the waiting Christmas trees of the flanked trucks.

What ya know, crazy Cherrik! Haven't seen you since around Omaha. I guess you heard what happened to Scotty later. Yeah, right on a hilltop in Texas, driving a pipe truck north of San Antone. The pipes shifted forward when he hit. How's it making, Cherrik? Me, I'm with Keeshin. I'd like to stay around, but I got to make like a train. Something the Air Force wants yesterday. We got it out of Cincinnati last night. Some kind of testing stuff. How's all the kids, Cherrik? Me? Oh, Midge called it off. No home life, she says. I get to see the kids every once in a while, whenever I get down to St. Louis.

Then the dawn slap of the screen door and the big Diesel warming up. Crunch of gravel under the duals and the old friend goes down the highway, climbing up through the gears until he is a far drone against the morning.

Twenty-one years and a lot of them had gone quietly and a lot of them had gone violently, but the violent separations were small in number, very small, compared to the ones killed in the cars, the small fragile, bug-quick cars that sped by his big rig, taking insane chances. It made him nervous to drive or ride in a car. It was too close to the road, and the skin of it was too thin, the horses too eager.

In the big rigs ice could kill you. Ice and hills. Fire could kill you. If one of the bright leaping crazy cars hit you head on it could kill you. But most times, in bad trouble, if you rode the rig you'd come through it.

But there had to be an end to it. Reflexes slowed down. Traffic moved at faster tempo. Yes, the rigs were bigger and quicker and more powerful, but that didn't help when the quickness needed was that of the strong wrist on the wheel. It would be time to go inside. Normal working hours. Regular food. Not so much fried stuff. He wondered if he'd be any good at all off a truck. They kept telling him they could use him.

He wondered if Quin-State would install the new gimmick on all the rigs this year. There was a lot of talk about it. A sealed meter that would give a complete history of each trip. Maximum speed, average speed, number of stops. Then the statistician in the chief dispatcher's office would analyze it and from that they would determine the best routes, the ablest drivers. Cherrik hoped he would be off the rigs before those things were installed. Even with your helper asleep in the bunk in back of your head you still felt alone on the high cold mornings droning through the sleeping towns. The dashboard bug would kill that feeling.

"Cherrik, the trip record shows that you decelerated sharply four miles south of Vernon, came to a dead stop and then continued."

"Did I come in on schedule?"

"Yes, but I want an answer to that question."

"What difference does it make?"

"Why, Cherrik, did you come to a dead stop on the open highway at six-seventeen on Tuesday morning?"

"Well, it was on account of a quail. She had a mess of little quail, about seven of them. They were crossing the road in single file and you see, I just happened to notice them ahead and . . ."

"Cherrik, you removed eleven dollars and three cents' worth of rubber, put unnecessary wear on the brakes and drove above maximum recommended speed in order to regain your schedule. The next time, Cherrik, I suggest you . . ."

No, you would not be completely alone again in the cab, not with the bug watching you with bland dial and moving scriber.

He slowed for the town of Blanchard, touching the brakes skillfully, watching to be certain no one was following too close. He shifted down through the gears, gauging the timing of the light ahead, alert for any kind of trouble on any side of him. He loafed and when the first light changed he mentally begged the car ahead of him to roll quickly, saving two more gear changes. It pulled away fast and a bulging orange wildcatter shouldered around him and into the lane in front of him. Cherrik looked at the weary rig with mild interest and no annoyance. He could not afford annoyance. He saw the collection of battered license plates and saw how deep and heavy the truck was on its suspension.

Scared to death of running into a check point, he guessed. Owner-driver, sweating out a mortgage on the rig, driving twenty hours a day, fighting for every salvageable second, becoming a bully of the road through pure desperation and weariness. He'd dope himself with no-sleep pills, and then spend a few hours twitching and moaning when he did get a chance to sleep. He'd grab off contracts at dawn markets, bidding starvation prices, and then hit the road, cursing the big outfits with their rotation of drivers, maintenance terminals, safety rules and slogans. He'd drive himself haggard, and drive his truck to breakdown or worse. And then they would close him out.

His only hope was to land a good regular contract. Then on the basis of that he would go in hock for a second rig and hire a driver and keep driving the old one himself. If he was one man in fifty thousand he might make it. Then he could sit in an office and his trucks would carry his name around the country. Then he would become virulent about rules and safety and programs. But now he was a menace, a man fighting for life and justification.

Cherrik sighed. Life was too short to get mixed up in that sort of thing. The orange truck pulled away, punishing the gears. It barely got through the second light on the caution signal. Cherrik had planned on making that light and would have made it had not the truck passed him when it did. But he could not afford irritation and annoyance. Anger killed lots of people. The sun was shining. He was ahead of schedule. Traffic was heavy, but the new road clicked the miles off effortlessly.

When the light changed he got all the mass of the big truck into motion, gaining speed smoothly, taking mild pleasure in his own skill. On the back of every Quin-State truck was the legend, "It's *your* road." He drove that way.

He was in the far right lane, the orange truck far ahead of him, two other trucks well back of him when he sensed trouble starting.

His mind quickened and took a picture of the scene almost as detailed and perfect as a camera could take. Straight, six-lane divided highway. On this particular stretch all lanes in fast use. Fairly wide gravel shoulder to the right of him and then a deep dangerous drop beyond it where a concrete wall retained the fill. He saw all that in the instant that a flicker of motion off to his left and well ahead of him told him trouble was coming.

Cherrik had a box seat for disaster. He saw the Cad leap and roll like a fish and his throat tightened as he saw the inevitable trajectory toward the oncoming cars. He knew then that whatever happened would be fatal for someone. He was pressing on the brake then, shifting down hard, trying to master the momentum of the truck as quickly as possible.

He saw the maroon car behind the blue convertible seem to hesitate and then dart forward, aiming for the hole between the vaulting tail of the blue car and the oncoming nose of the center lane car he had just passed. Cherrik saw what the maroon car was trying to do and pleaded with the fool in the center lane to drop back or move out to make more room. But the driver was frozen.

The maroon car hit the tail of the Cad a glancing blow, spinning it more certainly on its way. The maroon car, deflected by the blow, angled across the highway, missing the center lane car by an impossible fraction of an inch. The maroon car angled directly toward the front left wheel of Cherrik's big rig. He was not slowing fast enough to give it time to go by. If he kept his course he would hit it, roll it, smash it, catch up with it again and grind it into the road. He saw a girl's face in the right window of the car, looking up at him, her mouth wide.

Cherrik locked the truck wheels and turned the big wheel hard right. He saw, too late, that the concrete wall ended a few feet further, that he might have tried to hit the wide shoulder in just such a way that he would get past the bitter edge of the concrete into the clear and open field beyond. He thought, as the locked truck slid and hit: Too much time staring at the pretty girl, Cherrik. Too much dreaming. Too old, Cherrik. Too damn old.

chapter 7

SOME thoughts on the question of mass and momentum: A body in motion tends to stay in motion. A warm, soft, fragile body encased in sheet metal and traveling at a high rate of speed will continue to travel at that same rate of speed though the metal shell stops abruptly.

Problem for the class. Place our fragile young lady in the front seat of a car. Said car is traveling at the rate of sixty miles per hour. Place her twin sister, equally winsome, on the edge of the roof of an eleven-story building. See how tiny she looks up there? She smiles and waves at us.

Now place the dashboard of an automobile on the sidewalk, flat against the sidewalk. We are ready for our experiment.

At the same moment as we stop all forward motion in the moving vehicle, so that the young lady continues on at a velocity of ninety feet per second, her twin sister leaps from the roof of the building, head first, chin high, arms at her sides, descending with fluttering skirt and admirable accuracy directly onto the prone dashboard, ivory forehead impacting enameled metal.

Post mortem discloses to us that the young ladies suffered hurt of identical intensity. In both cases mass and momentum were equal, and thus the foot-pounds of force involved were also fearfully equal.

Hence the time-worn expression of "suicide seat," as it refers to the seat beside the driver.

Another example? Take your shiny new child of Detroit to the roof of the same eleven-story building, request that the sidewalk be roped off, then ease it over the edge and stand clear. Do it cleverly enough so that it lands precisely on its nose. Stenographers in the office windows may say "ah" as it descends. Then request your brother-in-law to drive the same model of car and indulge in a head-on collision with both vehicles traveling at a rate of precisely thirty miles an hour.

The damage to your car as compared to his? Identical.

Now imagine yourself to be quick enough and strong enough to walk up to the lady of your choice, put your arms around her and lift her off the floor at a velocity, achieved immediately, of ninety feet per second.

Her shoes, having mass of their own, would remain right there on the floor where she had been standing.

State troopers find many empty shoes, still laced, on the floors of twisted cars.

The tricks of mass and momentum are intriguing.

Mass and momentum are generous maidens. They always give you a bit more than you expect. Car skins are thin. Were they made to withstand the strain of fast impact—and they could be—engines in use could not move them, nor road beds support them.

At Mach 1 plus, impact can turn the pilot's body into a smear on metal one molecule thick. Such equations carry the effect of our two maidens far beyond sanity.

It is within their more ordinary realm, dealing with a million chromium grills, that we know them best.

Were they to kill with undeviating certainty, the sport would be taken out of it. If effect should always be equal to cause, all traffic would be decorous—tin snails in cautious file.

But the maidens are capricious. A car is tumbled in bloody ruin into an arroyo and presently a young man climbs unscratched from the heaped dead. Badly dazed, he wears a vague, apologetic smile, a smile of entreaty, in the same order as the tentative tail-waggings of the apologetic puppy. He fingers torn pants and is confused. A young girl in another place is thrown through a whirling canvas top and into a tall locust tree. After the whoof of flame, pale in the sunlight, the birds scold her and she is afraid to climb down from such a tall tree.

It is in these ways of caprice that the maidens tell us, clearly, that we have nothing to fear. For it will always happen to others, never to you and to me. Should the equation ever be weighted against us by a power of ten thousand to one, we will be thrown clear.

And so thirty thousand a year are harvested. (Insurance procedures deal with these dead quite readily, as death has a traditional value. It is the maimed who distress adjusters because judgments are often based on the number of years of life expectancy times the earning power which at one time had been anticipated. Death is neater, cheaper—and the forms are not difficult to fill out.)

The maidens have little sense of drama. As instruments of fate, they have no knack of selection. They kill indiscriminately the brave, the stupid, the young, the sick, the intelligent, the healthy, the cowardly, the old. The flesh of the careful driver tears as readily as the flesh of the fool, though perhaps not quite as often.

Of late, despite their clumsiness with plot, the maidens have been given wider stages. In the older, narrower theaters a mass of four or six tons and velocities from thirty to sixty had to satisfy them. Now, on broad sets, unique combinations of mass and momentum can be obtained, dealing with scores of tons and velocities up to a hundred and fifty feet per second.

On these stages there are no good, no bad—only the lucky.

At one-nineteen P.M. on Monday, May seventeenth, Trooper Shedd, driving amid the customary clot of tamed traffic, Trooper Christie beside him, eastbound, sat higher on the seat, narrowing his eyes.

"We got a beaut," he said to Christie. As he accelerated he snatched the mike from the dashboard rack and called in. He was closer, and he had made estimates before. "Five miles west of Blanchard. Bad. I'm not to it yet. Maybe five cars. Shake everybody loose who's anywhere near here. Ambulances. Fire." He touched the siren as he came closer. The sound of a siren seemed to settle them down. Traffic control was going to be the toughest part. He began to plan his campaign before he was out of the car.

chapter 8

THERE was the sound of busy traffic. And then the sudden hard yell of brakes which came at first from a single car and then was joined by the brake yells of the others. The crash was like a great slow thick-throated coughing sound containing bright sharp fragments in abrupt frequencies. As the initial sound of the crash passed its greatest peak, yet before it had died away, the second crash built it back to a yet higher intensity. Then, in diminuendo came the lesser impacts, descending to the recognizability of clash of fenders, rip of white metal. The quake of the shock quivered the roadside trees. Meadow birds circled wildly, crying out.

John Backum, factory representative, saw the road turn wild in front of him. He wrenched at the wheel, braked into a dry skid, teetered on the edge of control, touched the accelerator delicately after he had slid onto the gravel shoulder. The car lurched and straightened out and he drove along open pavement, his face suddenly wet, knees hollow, hands cramped with strain. An inch. Maybe less than an inch. The momentum of the car drifted it along. He gave it a little bit of gas. He tried to look back. He could not see anything.

He kept going. A thought kept nagging at him and he tried to answer it. Finally he answered it aloud. "Nothing I could do. Not a thing." The distant cry of a siren made him feel better.

He pulled into a gas station. When the attendant came over he said, "There's just been a hell of a crash back there a mile or so. I damn near got clobbered."

The dull-eyed attendant refused to be impressed. While his tank was being filled Backum went into the men's room. Before he left he found himself staring intently at his face in the mirror.

Herbert Merrit, with wife beside him, children and too much luggage in the rear seat, was worrying about the new job, the rented house, the reliability of the moving company, when traffic ahead of him broke up into crazy, hurtling, jagged projectiles. A black Ford spun around directly in his path. Off to his left there was a massive crash and a big blue car rebounded, upside down, angling toward him. His reactions froze and he sped by the spinning Ford, miraculously passing it when the long dimension of it was parallel to his own car. Something thudded the right rear corner of his car solidly as he went through.

He drove several hundred feet and pulled off on the shoulder. The children were yelping with excitement and staring out the rear window. Bobby rolled the side window down and leaned out so he could see better.

His wife was trembling. "Drive on, Herb. Please drive on. I don't want the children to see it."

"I've got to see what the damage is."

He got out and looked at the right rear. The fender was banged in against the wheel and the hub cap was dented and the corner of the bumper was bent out and torn. He looked back. The Ford he had missed had spun all the way across the road and had come to rest against a light pole. The skid had rubbed two tires off the rims. The door had burst open and a woman lay with her feet up among the pedals and her head near the base of the pole. She didn't look like a woman at all. He thought she looked like a dummy or a rag or something.

His wife called him and he got back in the car. He wondered about the legal aspects of leaving the scene of an accident. But it certainly wasn't as though it were a deserted road. He heard the siren and looked back and saw the police car.

"Please," his wife said. "Please." He drove on. The kids kept looking as long as there was anything to see.

Ben Hester had driven home to lunch in Blanchard and he was on his way back to the lumberyard. He was a hundred yards behind the blue Cad when he saw it leap the curbing, out of control. He glanced behind him as he put on the brakes. The road was clear behind him. As he braked, he saw the inevitable development of catastrophe. The blue car bucked and dug the right corner into the earth in the center strip. Ben saw the maroon Plymouth behind the Cadillac fighting for control and room. The center lane car didn't see or didn't understand the emergency. The Plymouth smacked the rear end of the Cadillac a glancing blow as it tried to eel through the gap. He saw it miss the center lane car, passing in front of it, and rocket directly toward a big semi. By then he was close enough to see it too well. The truck driver turned off. The maroon Plymouth went prancing and bouncing out into the wide fields. The truck nose dropped, drove hard into the concrete wall, sledged off a massive piece of it. Cab, trailer and broken wall fell ten feet, trailer telescoping the cab and then settling over onto its side propped up at an angle against the broken wall.

Ben Hester did not see what happened in the lanes on the far side of the highway. He knew it was bad and at the moment he did not care. He left his car and ran for the cab of the big semi. Any man who did what that driver had done, did it so deliberately, deserved every chance anybody could give him.

Joanna Bergson, driving her father's pickup truck, saw what happened in the eastbound lanes. She put on her brakes the moment it began. She saw the catapulting Cadillac nudged by a westbound car behind it. She saw the brown Chrysler, traveling very fast, sideswipe the black Ford and spin it away before smashing head on into the shark lunge of the heavy convertible. She saw the green Oldsmobile, trapped, try to cut left around the brown Chrysler and add its impact to the helpless length of the blue convertible. The blunt smash of the Chrysler had halted the momentum of the convertible. The Olds hit it and the force of impact tripped the Olds over so that it rolled once, end for end and twice on its side, balancing as though by intent on the center strip before coming to rest on the left side. The Cadillac, torn free of the crumpled Chrysler by the impact of the Olds, slid upside down out across the center lane. With wheels locked, the pickup slid forward and gave the upside-down car a final gentle nudge as they both came to rest. She had seen the skitter and twist of the cars which managed to shy away from impact. The brake sounds still continued behind her. There was a gnash of fenders and a banging of bumpers and then the sounds were gone. Cars pulled over onto the shoulder. Flame bloomed along the hood of the green Olds. She backed away from the upside-down car. She stopped and sat there, her face in her hands, motor running.

Transcription from tape:
Blue: What is this, anyway? I don't want to get mixed up in any kind of law stuff. I don't want to talk into this thing.

Garrard: This won't be used in any civil or criminal action. I'm from the State Highway Commission. We want to know how and why this thing happened. I'm interviewing several people. Trooper Shedd told me you saw how it happened. He also said you did a good job, helping.

Blue: I did what I could.

Garrard: Could I have your name, occupation, and reason for travel, please.

Blue: Daniel J. Blue. I'm heading east. I got that big GMC you maybe saw outside the station here. I'm with Felio Brothers Construction Company. We finished a job and we're moving the equipment to a new job near Providence. I sit high in that thing so I got a pretty good look. But I didn't see exactly how it happened.

Garrard: What did you see?

Blue: Well, the first thing I saw was that blue Caddy convertible jumping across the center strip. I don't know how he got out of control, and I don't know how it happpencd that truck cracked up over there or that Plymouth got the hell and gone out in that field. I just saw this side. The Caddy came over right into a mess of fast traffic. He come right at that Chrysler. The Chrysler tried to dodge and smacked the Ford and then sloughed into the Caddy. The guy behind the Chrysler had no place to go. He tried to cut around to the left and piled right into the same mess and went rolling down the middle. That Ford was spinning and everybody managed to miss it and then it smacked that pole.

Garrard: Would you say the speed of the cars involved was excessive?

Blue: I couldn't say. I think that Chrysler was boiling along pretty good. I think the others were about average. If you fellows want something to blame, how about that curb on the center strip?

Garrard: What did you do?

Blue: I stopped my truck and got out and ran toward the green Olds. I ran right by a girl in a pickup who'd come awful close to trouble. I figured the Olds needed help most because the fire started there. I got up on it and got the door open. There was a guy trying to get out. He acted like he didn't know where he was. I helped him out and he slid down over the curve of the roof and fell, but he got up okay. There were two others in there. One was a girl. Nobody made a damn move to come help me. I got her wrist and pulled until I got a look at her head. Then I let her go because I knew looking at her that there wasn't any point wasting time on her. It started getting damn hot. I got hold of the guy but he was wedged in. I think he was wiggling a little. I can't be certain. Then it just got too damn hot. I couldn't stand it. I had to get off there. That's when I got burned. A guy came up with a little bit of a fire extinguisher. It did about as much good as if he . . . (deleted from transcription).

Garrard: What happened then?

Blue: The troopers come about that time. One of them started getting traffic straightened out so the ambulances and fire wagon could get in. The other one and I started taking the people out of the Chrysler and laying them out on the road. The trooper got sick before we got the last one and then the first ambulance came, and more troopers. I figured everything was under control. I was going to get back in my truck and see if I could get out of there. Then my face started to hurt and after I got a look at it, I went back to see those ambulance guys.

Recommendations appended to accident report submitted by Trooper Shedd:

1. It is recommended that heavy duty jacks be carried by all road patrol cars. Such jacks would have been invaluable in conducting rescue operations in regard to the driver of the Quin-State truck.

2. It is recommended that the bad accident signs set out by converging patrol cars be placed at an angle between the middle and left lane of three-lane divided highways so as to aid in keeping the left lane clear.

3. It is recommended that some form of official letter or commendation be given to Mr. Daniel Blue, address on file at Station Eight, for his assistance in the rescue operations.

"You've got to give him a good talking to, George. I told him he had to stay in his room until you got home and we had a chance to talk about it. He was on his way back to school after lunch when that terrible accident happened down there on the highway. He and that Schwartz boy turned around and ran all the way back to the accident. My goodness, you could hear it all over the place. The first thing I thought was the chimney at the pipe plant had fallen down. Anyway, they had to hang around there, looking bug-eyed at all the blood and gore and dead people until the last dog was hung.

"I don't suppose that's too unnatural for kids, but they picked up this camera. See, it isn't a very good one, but they shouldn't have taken it. He says the Schwartz boy found it in the grass and it was thrown out of one of those cars and probably belonged to one of those poor people. He seems to think it's some kind of souvenir or something and I can't get it through his head that it's no different than stealing. They didn't go back to school at all, and I guess there were plenty others who didn't. I walked down to see what happened, but it made me feel sick and the crowd was so big I didn't see the boys there.

"You've got to give him a talking to, George, and you've got to take this camera somewhere, to the police or somebody."

chapter 9

THE blue convertible was bounding, lifting, turning. The seat tilted at an unreal angle, down toward the empty passenger's seat. Centrifugal force of the spin was thrusting him away from the wheel.

He sensed a strange helpless dreaminess. It was like being asleep and sensing that you are asleep. Through the fuzziness of mind came the shrill knowledge: This is bad! This is deadly! This can kill you! Kill meant death and death meant Gina, and that knowledge muted terror before it began.

There was even time to wonder at the strange slowness of this disaster that was happening at seventy miles an hour. And time to almost believe that the floating car would touch the other dream cars and rebound lightly, like balloons on a New Year's ceiling.

The sharp shock against the rear of the big car distorted its pattern of flight. The shock ripped Devlin Jamison's hands from the wheel and he was thrown headlong into the air. The car had been traveling straight. When the front right corner dug into the earth in the center strip, the car had been wrenched toward the left and, rebounding, began to tip over. The hundred and eighty pounds that was Devlin Jamison was a mass that tried to continue on in the line of original flight, so that when his hands were torn free, the paths of car and man diverged.

He flew in a long breathless airless moment—in a bright still place in time, the last slipping grip of his fingers imparting a slow spin to his body, so that in the deafened silence the unheard jangle of the highway wheeled slowly around him, opposed by the silent blue sky. The great crash of collision awakened all the stilled sounds, all the screaming of tires, and he sucked his heart small in readiness for the brute smash against man-made stone.

He struck flat on his side, on arm, shoulder, head, hip, thigh, calf, struck at a long flat angle against the earth of the center strip so that his body rebounded, struck again, slid, and rolled over and over out onto the concrete of the east-bound lane, limp hands flailing and slapping the stone, coming to rest with one leg canted up against the curbing of the center strip. He lay on his back, one arm across his throat. He put his hand down and felt the wetness of his fingers against the rough warmth of the concrete.

He got up with a stumbling, sick-legged eagerness. He took two steps and his toes hit the curbing and he fell face down on the grass. He opened his eyes. He could see the sun and shadow in among the grass roots. He remembered when he was little, stretching out in just this way, adjusting to the tiny grass world until an ant was as big as he was, and the stems were the smooth green trunks of tropical trees. There was a small red ribbon in the grass. He looked at it for a long time before he realized, quite suddenly, that it was one of those strips of red cellophane from the top of a pack of cigarettes.

He wished there were something else to look at and wonder about. He wanted to puzzle over some small thing. Then he would not have to begin to think of his body and how his body felt. And he would not have to think of what he would see in the highway.

He lay there and listened to the world around him. There were far-off traffic sounds, but no sounds near by. There was an undertone of low voices. A man shouted. There was a siren, which died close by. Car doors thudded. There was a crackling sound, and a smell of greasy burning. There was a sharp tinkle as a last piece of glass fell to stone.

Bert Scholl saw the blue car in the lunging, driving fall that took it at an angle across his path. He saw the driver thrown. The car had turned toward him so that in a vivid moment before he smashed into it, he could see into the open convertible, see the wheel and upholstery. One of the girls, thrown forward by his savage jab at the brakes, pressed hard against his head and shoulders.

He saw that he would hit the car right about at the windshield. It seemed a funny damn place to smash into a car. He had a clear sharp moment of anger. Damn fool in his big car, bouncing all over the damn highway.

There was a fractional second of bitter regret for the vacation spoiled, the car smashed. No Whiteface Mountain, no North Pole, no Frontier Town, no Ausable Chasm, no Streamline Ferry.

The bitter regret had just begun to change, in the incredible microseconds of the mind, to fear when the two cars struck with the greatest sound in all the world.

He was braced for impact. He willed the powerful arms and wrists to resist impact. But impact did not come to him as a great blow. There seemed a softness about it. He watched a tiny blazing white figure set against deep blackness. He saw that the little figure was himself, sitting, hands held as though he grasped a wheel. It moved away from him, still in that same position, going further and further away, getting smaller and brighter. It was like the little glowing spot that shrinks when you turn the television off. It went so far away he could not see it any more.

Cherrik felt the shock as the wheels folded back and then the frame chunked into the wall and hammered the great slab of wall loose. He felt the sickening drop and in the moment of falling, he was aware of all the tons behind him, falling with him. The tractor struck and canted up and he was jammed forward into darkness.

He opened his eyes. He could hear voices. The cab was tipped over toward the left and it had a crazy look. The angles were all wrong. The windshield was tilted forward so that all he could see through it was the red top of the hood. The glass was cracked in a thousand crazy directions, and bulged so that some jigsaw pieces had fallen out of it. He was all jammed up into the front left corner of the cab, his nose a few inches from the shattered glass. He could look down toward his left and see raw ripped earth about a foot below the open side window. He could turn his head a little bit. He turned it toward the right and saw that the other window just wasn't there. The cab had been squeezed shut on that side. He could hear faraway voices. He kept trying to remember what he was carrying, where he had been going, how a thing like this had happened.

Breathing bothered him. He could take little short breaths, high up in his lungs. The weight against his back and the weight against his chest kept him from breathing. He tried to cough but it was a sick little "kih-kih" sound.

He tried to move his left arm. It was clamped down somehow between his side and the door. He could wiggle his fingers but that was all. He could move his right arm, but it hurt. It hurt like nothing he had ever felt before. He moistened his lips. He wondered what the voices were talking about. They ought to quit the chatter and get him out of here. He wondered about his legs. He tried to move them and couldn't feel anything. He couldn't even tell what position they were in. Panic began to rise within him, but he pressed it back. Hell, he was just being squeezed so tight his legs had gone numb. Perfectly natural.

There was a smooth hard thing under his chin. He rubbed his chin against it and realized it was the upper edge of the steering wheel. He wished he could remember where he had been headed. It was funny to have something like this happen and not know anything about it. Not even remember if there'd been a helper along when . . . He felt weak and sick. If a helper had been asleep back there, he wouldn't have had a chance. Not the way the cab was buckled and squeezed nearly shut.

He heard a clink of metal near by. He decided to yell. It was a discouragingly feeble effort. He couldn't make a breath last long enough to yell the way he wanted to. He tried three times. Suddenly a face appeared right beside him, upside down against the raw torn dirt. It was a stranger.

"Look, we're trying to get the load off your back, Pop. How you feel? I was down here before and you were taking a nap."

"It's awful damn . . . tight in . . . here."

"Here's the picture. Your trailer is hanging by a whisker. There's two tow trucks getting lines on it so it won't slip. We get that anchored, and we'll take torches and cut you out of here. Just sit tight. Don't go away, Pop."

"Wait . . . wait a minute. What happened?"

"A guy that saw it says you took the ditch when a car got knocked right in front of you. It was just a hell of a big ditch, Pop. Look, I'll see if I can get one of those medics to crawl down in here and have another look. They don't like the look of it down here much."

"I'm . . . okay. Just . . . hurry up and . . . get the load off me."

"Sure thing." The face was gone.

He remembered how it had happened. He remembered the load, the schedule, the destination. He wished he'd asked the young fellow how the passenger car made out. He remembered the girl's face. Just a glance, but a nice face. Scared, too. He hoped she and her boy friend made out all right.

There was another metallic sound and he heard the thin grind of a winch. They knew what they were doing out there. He felt a faint tremor in his shoulders as the load shifted a fraction of an inch.

Hell of a thing. The tractor was junk. Probably the trailer too. First rig he'd ever washed out. He'd chopped one up pretty bad, years ago. Hydraulic line broke on a steep grade, went out so fast he hadn't had time to work her down through the gears. Town at the foot of the hill. So he'd waited until there was a gap in the guard railing on the right. He'd wheeled it into the gap and straightened it out. The truck had busted off damn near a hundred reinforced concrete posts, and wadded up a big bale of steel cable underneath before it had come to a reluctant stop. They hadn't classified that as an accident. The old man had given him a bonus for that.

Anyway, it was good to know he'd been alone on this run. And then he suddenly couldn't remember where he had been headed. He moistened his lips and tried to think. Funny thing to be so light-headed. He wished he could feel his legs. The way he was jammed up in the corner, they might be broken all to hell. They might be bleeding and he'd never know it.

They were yelling orders up there somewhere. And somebody yelled, "Watch it!"

The winch was whining again. The load trembled again. He heard a crumpling, tearing sound. He was scared. He wan'ed to be home. He bit at his mouth and started to cry. The load trembled. A tow truck was pulled sideways a few inches. The load slid forward a full twelve inches and came to rest again.

When it was safe to check, the young man went down again, sliding down on his back on the moist earth. He looked and then worked his way out. He stood up and looked at the sky and then suddenly hammered his fist against the metal skin of the trailer.

The girl had been bored and restless. It had seemed like fun, just taking off when Charlie asked her. Jeanie would be sore. She would have been able to come too, if this Jim type had been fun, like Charlie. She wished Charlie would wake up. Jim talked funny. They seemed to have plenty of money. It was a nice car. But the way Jim talked, it could be stolen. That would be a hell of a note. There hadn't been much liquor, and now it was gone. If Jim didn't pick a place to stop pretty soon, she was going to bust.

This was beginning to look as if it had been a pretty tired idea. If the law wanted them and grabbed them, it could be a real mess.

Maybe when Charlie woke up it would be fun again. Charlie did and said funny things. He just didn't seem to give a damn about anything. This Jim acted as if he was better than other people. Anyway, it was better than not going anyplace. This would have been a day like any other. Sleep late and fool around in the cabin washing out stuff and mending stuff, then go over on the beach at the lake in the afternoon and see who was there, and wind up at Red's with the same old faces.

She yawned and stretched. Then she folded her arms on the back of the front seat again, maliciously keeping her elbow firmly against Jim's shoulder. She looked down. Charlie certainly looked dead to the world. He looked younger with his eyes closed. Like a kid.

She watched drowsily ahead as they came up behind a new Ford in the center lane, hung there while a brown Chrysler went by on their left, and then swung out. Jim could certainly handle a car. It had been nice last night, in the back seat with Charlie while Jim drove so smoothly through the darkness.

The brown Chrysler ahead of them jammed on the brakes. Jim hit the brakes too, so hard that she banged forward against the back of the front seat, hurting her breasts. The Chrysler banged the Ford which had caught up with it again and she began to scream as she saw that they were going to pile into the back end of the Chrysler. Jim swung around the Chrysler, bouncing high and hard on the curbing. She saw another car in the way, coming at them, and saw a man fly toward them, going right over the top of the car.

She was still screaming when they hit. Jim had dropped down below the seat somewhere. They hit and she felt the hard lunge of her body and saw the rear vision mirror swooping right up toward her eyes. The last thing she saw was her own round wide blue staring eyes before. . . .

Suzie Scholl had been lost in a distant daydream, unaware of the traffic, of her family—dimly conscious of the fact that she was riding in a car. The quick shock of the brakes slammed her forward so that she lifted out of the seat and banged her arm against her father's shoulders, her head against the back of his neck. The force of deceleration kept her pinned there, unable to push herself back. She could smell the stuff he used on his hair. She saw her mother braced against the dashboard, and saw Connie more than halfway over into the front seat, thin legs waving. She could not see ahead. The car swerved and she heard the bang as it hit something on the right.

Then the force eased a bit. Just for a fraction of a second. They hit. It was a great smashing thud that drove her father forward, drove her forward with him, scraping her forcibly over the top of the seat so that she slid off his shoulder banging the top of her head against the dashboard and sliding down onto the floor, face down, legs up and back. It felt as if the whole world had jumped up into the air and fallen with a broken crash. There was a thing in her mind like a black shade. Something had hold of it and kept pulling it almost all the way down, leaving only a crack to see out of. She would push it up. It was very heavy. They would pull it down again. Things made hot crinkling sounds and there was a smell of hot oil. Something hot was flowing along her loins, running down the slant of her body.

She held the black shade away and opened her eyes. Her shoulders were against the car floor, her head twisted to the side, the brake pedal digging into her cheek below her eye. She could look up at her father. She could not see his face; it was too far forward, beyond the curve of the dash. The steering wheel was down around the steering post. The steering post disappeared into his body. Blood ran down along the steering post. The heel of her right foot was over the top of the seat. She could see her round bare thigh. There was a long open cut in it.

The black shade was pulled all the way down and she waited behind it. She waited in dark patience. Something dripped in the darkness. Hands took her and pain flashed before the darkness became thicker and softer.

Then her eyes hurt. She squinted her eyes open. She turned her head. There was a thing beside her. Where the pattern was caked dark, she could see the design of Connie's blouse. Little blue thistles on a white field. It wore Connie's blouse. But where the head should have been there was a thing as big as a head, but it looked like a raw joint torn from the hip of an animal. The shape was wrong. There were grainings of white.

Suzie tried to sit up. Hands forced her back down and a voice murmured something. After a long time she was moved carefully onto something and lifted. She opened her eyes. A lot of people were standing staring at her. She tried to smile at them. She was slid into darkness, and doors were closed. A man held her wrist. He wore a white coat. They went fast and a siren followed them. She realized after a time that it was their siren. They took her into a narrow place where there were a lot of people talking. A man watched while a nurse cut her clothing off. The man put a needle in her arm. The black shade came down hard.

As the crash came and Frazier was slammed forward against the fire wall, he had the horrid feeling that the motor was going to be driven back through to crush him. The car swung up and over. It swung and banged and circled. It felt to him as though something had picked it up to shake it. He tried to stay in place, but the motion hurled him out from under the dash. He banged on the roof and on the dash and on the side. The car turned, sighed, sagged and settled down. He was on his knees, arms cradling his head, a weight on his back. He took his arms away. He realized he was on his knees on the left rear door. He braced his arms and stood up and the weight fell away from him.

He felt weak and old. He could move slowly, fumblingly. He turned. The girl was near him. Charlie was on top of her. She was dead. Her brows and nose were crushed in. She was hideous. He plucked weakly at Charlie. Charlie moaned. Charlie was all tangled up with the girl, wedged in by the wheel.

A stocky man opened the door above him, leaned it back and put his weight on it until something broke and it opened down. He reached his hand in. Frazier took the hand and wiggled weakly out. He slid down over the top of the car, fell, and got up. The flames were hot. The man reached in the car and fumbled at the other two. He shielded his face from the heat, tried again and then jumped down from the car. Frazier saw that the left side of the man's face was blistered.

"I got a look at the woman," the man said. "She's dead."

"I know," Frazier said.

"I couldn't get the guy. It got too hot."

Frazier walked away and sat down on the grass. The man

went over toward the smashed Chrysler. Frazier saw the troopers. He felt his insides twist. He looked at the flames. The car burned hotly. He could not see into the car. He turned away and felt the flame heat against his ear. He listened to the flames. He looked at his hands. The knuckles of his left hand were barked. His jacket sleeve was torn open up to the elbow. His mouth was puffed, two lower teeth loosened.

When the sound of the fire changed he looked again. Two firemen were plastering the car with foam. The flames were smothered and they died. The undercoat had caught. It burned stubbornly, emitting a greasy smoke. A tow truck backed into position and a man put the hook around a frame member. The truck moved and the car tilted and fell down onto its wheels, bouncing loosely. The firemen moved close and one of them shined a flashlight into the smoky interior, playing it around. A trooper came over and the firemen said something to him. They both looked toward Frazier, walked over toward him.

Frazier looked at the ground. They stood over him.

"Were there just two others in the car?" the trooper asked.

"Yes."

"Can you give me the names, please."

"I don't know the names."

"How come?"

"I was hitching a ride. They picked me up about a hundred miles back. A man and a woman. I guess they were man and wife. They talked that way."

"Who was driving?"

"The man was. I was asleep in the back. I guess that's why I didn't get killed."

"You were damn lucky to come out of that. I'll send one of the doctors over. Don't try to get up."

"I'm all right."

"You didn't see how it happened?"

"I don't know what happened. I was asleep."

The trooper went away. Frazier tried to force himself to think clearly. They would check the Florida plate. But even before they found the plate was no good they might check in the back end. A little heat wouldn't have hurt the Positive and the .357 Magnum. In fact, had it gotten too warm in the trunk compartment, the ammunition would have started to pop. That meant the clothes would be recognizable enough. Clothing for two men of different sizes. No woman's clothing. Improper registration and a couple of guns. Enough reason to grab hold of one Frazier and put him on ice until they could find out what went on. He took his wallet out and looked through the bills. About eighty dollars.

And there was about forty thousand in the trunk compartment, wadded inside the extra spare tire. Nobody was likely to find it there. Not right off. He began to think more clearly. Percentage said to get lost in this crowd. Stay in the area. Find out where the car would be taken. It was junk now. It would be stripped after the police took the luggage. Drop around to whatever garage it landed in and make a fair offer for the spares. Both of them. That would look better than trying to get the right one.

It had seemed like the worst kind of luck. But things began to look a little better. Charlie had been too erratic lately. Sound on the job, but unpredictable otherwise. This broke it up. The girl was certainly no loss, to herself, or anyone else.

He stood up when the ambulance intern came over. "I want to check you over."

"I'm fine."

"You better let me take a look."

"I've got a good doctor of my own. If anybody looks at me, it's going to be him."

The man looked at him and shrugged. "Suit yourself, mister."

The torn coat was conspicuous. Frazier took it off and folded the torn sleeve inside and hung it over his arm. He went over to where two men with a tow truck were considering the problem of the upside-down convertible.

"Where'll these cars be taken?" he asked.

"Which one?"

"The green Olds. It was green. Hard to tell now."

"Ace Garage has got that one. Right in Blanchard. We'll hold it until the insurance gets straightened around, and make a bid on it. Damn small bid. Joe, let's run two lines right under it and bring them up the other side and hook on the frame. Then when we lift, she ought to roll over."

"Hurry up and get this thing off the road," a trooper said.

"Sure, sure," the tow truck man said bitterly.

Frazier heard another man go up to the trooper and say, "How many killed here, officer?"

"Three in the Chrysler and two in the Olds so far. They're trying to get the driver out of that truck but it don't look good, I understand. And that woman in the Ford was hurt bad, and the girl in the Chrysler didn't look good to me. So it could be anywheres from five to eight, Mr. Garrard."

Frazier moved away into the crowd. People were walking back to their cars. The troopers were getting the cars moving. The Chrysler had been taken away. The Ford had been moved further off the road. Two tow trucks were working on the big truck. He looked back and saw the shattered Cadillac fall back onto its wheels and rock. Frazier put cars between him and the troopers. He walked down the shoulder of the road toward Blanchard. He was stiff and sore in every muscle. His mouth hurt. He sucked at his barked fingers. Traffic began to move swiftly again. He lengthened his stride, working the stiffness out of his legs. With any kind of luck it would work. He'd been careful not to look up into the trooper's face. There ought to be some place to hole up in Blanchard. Throw the coat away and buy a different shirt. Hang around the Ace Garage. Move slow and easy, but, come what may, grab that tire.

The black Ford spun on the dry pavement. All sense of direction was gone. Cars were shadows that whipped by her and she clung to the wheel in momentary expectation of shock and death. Just as the wheels gained traction again, she saw the heavy pole beyond the shoulder of the road. She tried to steer away from it and felt the back end of the car swing again. It struck heavily against the pole and the door burst open and she was hurled out. In the final moment before the blackness, she felt acute irritation with the formlessness, the messiness of it. This was destruction and waste, devoid of pattern and meaning. She would be helpless among strangers.

chapter 10

FOR the fast through traffic, Blanchard was the annoyance of two traffic lights, a name half remembered. Route 56, however, touched only the south edge of the town. It was an old town, and it had grown up on the banks of a stream that wound down through a shallow north-south valley. In the beginning, when timber was heavy on the hills to the north, the stream had been a source of power. But as the hills were logged bare the water table changed and the stream became too meager. In the spring it often ran high, but in September and October it was quite often completely dry.

The first era of growth and prosperity came from the forests and the game and the stage line. After the forests and the game were gone, Blanchard became a trading center for the surrounding farms. For many years the wagons, and later the high square dusty cars, came down the dirt roads into Blanchard of a weekend, and merchants prospered.

With the improvement of roads, and the exhaustion of the surrounding land, Blanchard began to decay. Farmers preferred to make the longer trip to the city twenty-five miles away where the range of choice was wider. During this period the town shrunk to little more than two thousand inhabitants. Old houses stood empty and the pipe plant was the only industry.

But with further improvement of the east-west highway prosperity of a different sort began to return. The old stream had dried up, but now a river of dollars flowed endlessly by. With the completion of the super-highway the transition became complete. The new center of growth and vitality was at the south edge of the town, an area of motels, restaurants and large glossy service stations.

Nor did the old town remain unchanged. The city was now only thirty minutes away. Foresighted people of means began to buy the old houses at bargain prices and restore

81

them to their original pre-Victorian charm. Only the first few obtained bargain prices. As it became increasingly smart to move out to Blanchard, real estate prices moved steadily upward. Promoters purchased tracts of open land and built expensive ranch-style homes. As the population and the tax rolls increased, new money became available for schools and services. The grandsons of merchants faced old stores with plastic. A "city" group of professional and business people had moved into the town and changed its face.

The dividing line between the old residents and the new was sharply drawn, but as the young people of both groups began to mingle, the line of demarcation was becoming more fuzzy.

In some instances, in fact, a man who had moved his residence from the city to Blanchard would find it possible to change his place of business also. Such a man was Dr. Lionel Budischon. He had been one of the first who moved out to Blanchard and purchased one of the old houses. He had been a highly successful doctor in the city. As his father, before his death, had been the president of one of the larger banks and had served on the board of many local corporations, Budischon's social contacts had been, from the beginning, excellent and profitable. His first patients were the friends of childhood. As he began practice with splendid offices, personal charm and great assurance, his career was never in doubt. He performed general surgery, kept up a general practice, and tried sincerely to stay abreast of new advances in the field of medicine.

At the age of fifty, when he moved to Blanchard with his thirty-year-old second wife and two small children, he was a hearty, florid, balding man who played robust golf and shrewd poker. He left, back in the city, a young associate who took those night calls considered necessary. Budischon was a profane man and an obstinate man.

During his first year in Blanchard he realized he was discontented. He was worth nearly three hundred thousand dollars, had a lovely wife, pleasant children, cars, friends—but he felt unused by his profession. His patients were so uniformly well-to-do, outside of his regular clinic work, that in the case of anything serious, specialists were called in.

Once he had made up his mind, golf and poker were given up. The young associate was burdened with a great deal more of the practice. His wife and children saw less of him. He worked and planned and argued fourteen hours a day. At the end of that time a great deal of his money was gone. But on the piece of property adjoining his was the new trim pale green building, with letters in chaste aluminum saying "BUDISCHON HOSPITAL AND CLINIC."

It was tiny, but it was perfect. There were two six-bed wards and two three-bed wards in one wing, as well as four small private rooms. In the other wing there were twelve private rooms, nearly as luxurious as the rooms in a first-class hotel. The higher central portion of the building housed the clinic offices, laboratory, operating room, nurses' quarters.

It did not take long to acquire a small competent staff. In addition to Budischon and the nursing office staff, there was a radiologist, an internist, a urologist, a neurologist, a dermatologist and an anesthetist. The other doctors came to Blanchard to live. As it was a private institution, admissions could be kept down to the number of patients who could be adequately cared for. It was generally full. Budischon found within himself unsuspected talents as an administrator. He was completely busy and completely happy.

On the afternoon of May seventeenth, the girl at the switchboard received the police request for the dispatch of the hospital ambulance to the scene of the accident west of the city. Hearing that it was a multiple-car crash, the switchboard girl, after dispatching the ambulance, contacted the local funeral home of Reedy and Quell which supplied their two hearses to be used as ambulances in case of emergency. The head nurse was advised of the situation, and by the time the ambulance returned four beds were ready, as well as the emergency facilities of the small hospital.

Dr. Budischon met the ambulance and spoke to Dr. David Prace, the young doctor who had ridden to the scene of the accident. "How many, Dave?"

"Just three for us, but six customers for Reedy and Quell. It was a nasty one. I brought our three back in one load. Funny thing. There was a fourth one, a man, but he disappeared. And before I forget, there's a couple coming in to be checked over after they see to their car. They got shaken up and I took care of a laceration on the woman's knee. We've got a head injury and I suggest we get George to take some pictures of that right away."

Budischon watched them come in. He saw a woman in a torn, bloody, dark red suit, her dark blonde braided hair matted. There was a deep longitudinal laceration at the hairline and a great ugly contusion, the color of eggplant, covering most of the left side of her forehead. The eye was puffed completely shut. He saw that her features were regular and her skin good. The waste and pain saddened him. Disease was explicable to him. But not this smashing of healthy bodies. He saw the gleam of perspiration on her face, her grayish-yellow color. He stepped forward and felt the clammy chill of her hand, felt of the fast thready pulse.

"Treat her for shock," he ordered.

The second one was a young girl in the torn matted ruin of a yellow sweater and heavy white skirt. Her face was unmarked. She looked about in a dazed, placid way. Dave stopped beside him and said in a low tone, "She's got a hell of a rip in her thigh, broken left hand and wrist, dislocated shoulder and maybe some ribs snapped. Only one left out of a family of four. They really hit hard. Put the steering post through the driver, stuffed the mother halfway through the windshield and damn near beheaded her. Pulped the little sister's head. I don't know how or why this one came out of it. I'll get to work on her."

The last one was a big man with a strong heavy face. He was protesting, in a deep cultivated voice, that he was perfectly able to walk. His clothing, though badly damaged, looked expensive. The fingers of his right hand were bleeding. The lobe of his left ear was torn. Budischon spoke with curt authority and the man stopped objecting. This was the sort of accident patient you had to watch closely. There was so much raw animal energy there that, numbed by shock, such patients could walk around with incredible injuries, doing themselves much harm.

By four o'clock the last of the wet X-ray prints had been examined and the three unconscious patients, two of them under sedation, had been identified. Mr. Devlin A. Jamison, Miss Kathryn Aller, Miss Susan Ann Scholl. Mr. Jamison's split fingers had been treated, his ear stitched, the abrasions on the side of his face, on his hip, on his elbow and shoulder cleaned and bandaged. His cracked ribs had been taped, and his dislocated finger reset and given a temporary splint. He was in the best shape of the three. Dr. Budischon, wondering about a sedative, watched the man, saw the way he seemed to be suffering some great mental stress. After he had found out whom to phone, he prescribed a sedative.

He placed the long-distance call from his office at quarter after four, a person to person call to a Mr. Roger Seiver.

"Mr. Seiver, this is Dr. Budischon. I'm calling in regard to a Mr. Devlin Jamison."

At first Seiver couldn't get it through his head what had happened. Budischon explained his position in the matter. Seiver got very concerned.

"You say other cars were involved, Doctor?"

"Several, I understand."

"I guess Dev told you I'm his attorney. I better come out there. I'll be out some time tomorrow. In the meanwhile I'll contact the insurance agent. Thanks for calling."

Budischon felt slightly guilty as he hung up the phone. He knew that the State Police in their own good time would have made the necessary contacts. But Mr. Jamison looked like a man who would appreciate that little additional service. Dr. Budischon knew he had no intention of making any contacts for the other two patients. He sighed. Long years of service to the well-to-do led to minor forms of prostitution, disguised as personal favors.

He looked in on the Aller woman. The scalp laceration had been sutured. The contusion looked angrier than before. Plasma had removed the symptoms of shock. The nurse told him there was no change. The plates showed no fracture. He went to the bed and rubbed his thumb lightly across her eyelashes on the good eye, watching closely for any sign of reaction. There was none. She was in deep coma. At best it would be severe concussion. At worst—brain hemorrhage, a slow seeping of blood through torn tissues. He looked at the still figure and wondered who was waiting for her. Maybe somebody was, at this moment, beginning to worry. I wonder what can be holding Kathryn up. You'd think she'd at least phone.

He looked in on the Scholl girl last. She slept placidly. Her right arm and hand were in a cast. Her shoulder had been snapped back into place and strapped. Her broken ribs had been taped, and the deep laceration in the top of her thigh had been carefully sutured. The rip had gone deep enough to require deep stitches in the muscle tissue and to require the precaution of a drain. He had done the work himself, and he smiled as he thought how easily she would heal. Hers was a sturdy body fairly bursting with health. The smile faded. Mental and emotional hurt would not be so quick to heal.

When he got back to his office he found Lieutenant Fay of the State Police waiting for him.

"Hello, Doctor. What's the score on the accident?"

"Hi, Tommy," Budischon said, and sat down at his desk. "We've got one very sick lady. Your office called and gave us her name. Aller. Head injury. I don't know how serious yet. She's comatose. Jamison and the Scholl girl are doing fine."

"We got all the stuff out of the cars back at the barracks and we've been going through it to see what we could do about notifications. The Aller woman is a stopper. California plates, but enough stuff with her, personal stuff, so I'd guess she was moving east. But no indication of where she was going. The girl found some things that indicate she originally came from Philadelphia. She has a wallet in her purse with a card that says in case of accident notify somebody named Houde, president of some chemical company out there. But she was carrying a letter of recommendation from him saying she was quitting to come east. I don't know. We're stopped, I guess, until she can tell us who to notify. On Jamison, I have his home number, but we haven't been able to raise anybody."

Budischon coughed and said, "Mr. Jamison gave me the name of his attorney and I took the liberty of notifying him. I guess I should have phoned you and told you."

Fay, a heavy, freckled, red-haired man, gave Dr. Budischon a sharp look. "That's good service, Doctor. Thanks. And he'll probably need a lawyer."

"How so?"

"He jumped the center strip right into oncoming traffic. I've got an expert going over his car."

"How about the Scholl family?"

"That one was easy. He had a card in his wallet saying to get in touch with a fellow named Krissel. Turns out it's his brother-in-law. He'll get here tonight or tomorrow. The truck driver was easy too. The man at the trucking company offices said he'd contact the family and tell them the score. That's a nasty job I'm glad I don't have to do. I haven't told you the real package yet. It's the main reason why I stopped by."

"Some of the ones that were killed?"

"Yes. A pair of them. Man and woman. There were three of them in the car. One got out in good shape. A man. Did he show up here for treatment?"

"Not yet. And there's a couple who . . ."

"I know about them. This is a man about thirty, dark hair and eyes, gray sport jacket with a torn left sleeve, pale blue sport shirt, bruised mouth, scraped knuckles. No sign of him?"

"Not yet. Why?"

"He claimed to Shedd that he was a hitchhiker. The car burned with the other two inside it."

Budischon made a face of distaste. "I hadn't heard that."

"They burned good. We got the stuff out of the back end of the car. Clothing for two men. No clothes for a woman. And no signs that her clothes burned up inside the car. Just clothes, some purchased in Florida and some in Jersey. Not a single damn personal thing, unless you want to call safety razors personal. And two nice fat revolvers, Doctor. Loaded. And extra boxes of shells for both of them. We checked the license fast. It didn't belong on the Olds they were in. It belonged on a Studebaker that was smashed up a couple of months ago. Tallahassee says that car was a total loss. We've got the motor and chassis numbers on the Olds and my guess is that it will check out hot. The guy who got out of it refused to be looked at by your Dr. Prace. He just wandered off."

"What do you make of it?"

"Two sharpies in a hot car. And probably hot themselves. They picked up the girl someplace. They were headed east."

"Can the man in the car be identified?"

"Maybe by his teeth. I don't know of any other way." Fay stood up. "I thought I'd stop by and ask you to keep a look out for him. He may need attention. If he stops by, try to hold him here. Let me know. And expect some reporters on your tail, Doctor. They've already hit my shop. They know about the guns, and they've got their teeth into that. And they're already talking about the Aller woman as the mystery woman."

It was nearly five o'clock before the crushed body of Cherrik had been removed from the collapsed cab of the truck and taken to the back entrance of Reedy and Quell. The body was placed on the zinc-topped table in the middle of the small concrete room.

LaFleur leaned wearily against the wall and smoked a cigarette while Smith took the clothing off the body.

"You could help, couldn't you?" Smith said.

"You're doing fine, kid. Fine. Hose it down and then I'll see what we got here."

When Smith had finished LaFleur took a closer look at

the body. "There isn't a shot glass of blood left in this critter. But this won't be as bad as the fat woman was. It won't take long. It'll be a transfer too. What do you say we finish up now?"

Smith looked at his watch. "Might as well, I guess."

"This one is going to look just fine." He nudged Smith. "A lot better than three others I could mention, hey?"

"Knock it off," Smith said sullenly.

"Your attitude isn't right yet, kid."

"I said knock it off!"

"Now you take that burnt gal. You could still see she had a real good built."

"Shut up!"

"It's such a kind of waste, isn't it, kid? All that woman all used up all at once and poor Smith can't even get himself a date."

Smith gave him a look of hate and indignation and ran out of the room. LaFleur chuckled softly, stepped on his cigarette, and approached the work at hand.

Out at the scene of the accident men were transferring the load from the shattered truck trailer to a truck parked near by. Local people slowed down as they passed the place. Aside from the truck there was little to see. Scars gouged deep in the center strip, streaks of black rubber on the concrete, a darkened, scorched place, some small fragments of glass. At Station Eight were piles of luggage, neatly tied and tagged.

Twenty-five miles east, in the city, twine-tied bundles of the second evening edition were dumped off the route trucks at the corner stands. There was an item at the bottom of page one with a two-column head: "SIX KILLED IN HIGHWAY SMASH NEAR BLANCHARD." The subhead said, "TWO BODIES UNIDENTIFIED."

Five out-of-state cars and a truck were involved early this afternoon, six miles west of Blanchard, in a high-speed collision that took six lives and left five injured, one of them seriously. Officials term it the worst accident since the opening of the new highway three years ago. . . .

Neighbors filled the home of the Cherriks. Two of the women were in the bedroom with Sophie Cherrik. The men talked in the small living room, their voices slow, hushed, heavy.

A reporter named Steve Lanney waited patiently in his car outside the Budischon Hospital for a chance to talk to the doctor.

chapter 11

THEIR maroon Plymouth was in the Ace Garage and they had been told that if they came back by six the mechanics would have been over it and could then give an estimate of the amount of money and the time involved.

Paul sat with Joyce at a small table against a front window of a luncheonette diagonally across from the Ace Garage. Coffee cooled in front of him. He looked out at the traffic, waiting in impatient fuming glitter at the traffic light, the sun slanted low behind the buildings, dust opaque and golden where the sun came between the buildings. He felt as if he saw each small thing with a clarity he had never known before. And each small thing seemed weighted with symbolism, with meanings that reached far down into the texture of his mind. He saw a silver devil on the hood of a teen-age car, silver thumb to silver nose. And in that there was a referent point to himself. He saw a man, waiting for the light, make a delicate adjustment to his side mirror. He saw a square, brown, bored, insolent, civilized dog pause on the curb, flick wise eyes at light and traffic and trot across between the moving cars.

He looked at the tan burn-proof, stain-proof, chip-proof top of the luncheonette table and at Joyce's slim hand which rested there, fingers slightly curled. He saw the pore texture of the back of her hand, raised hint of tendon, tributary shadow of vein, unique whorls along the edge of the pad of her index finger. Her hand seemed the most clever and perfect and mysterious thing he had ever looked at. He had never looked at a hand before, at that strange instrument for grasping, for work, for caress.

Whenever he loosened his firm hold on his mind for an instant, he was transposed back to that moment of truth on the highway. He was back in the speeding car, aiming for the gap which was not opening fast enough. He felt again the shock as he struck the back of the blue car and ricocheted diagonally across the highway, out of control. He held

climbed up the hill. He wiped his hands on his pants. There was black dirt on his shirt.

"Are you the driver of the truck?" Paul asked. "I want to thank . . ."

"No. I'm not the driver. He's still in there. I think he's alive. Look at the cab. I don't know how the hell they'll get him out." He looked at Paul indignantly. "You were in the red car. I saw it. By God, that guy did you a turn."

"I know. But I couldn't help it. The blue car . . ."

"I saw that too. I saw the whole thing. That truck driver took the ditch to keep from killing the two of you." He looked at them with a hard bright stare of accusation. He turned and headed toward the troopers.

Paul and Joyce looked down at the crumpled cab below them. Joyce moved closer to him and took his hand. He turned and saw that the green car was burning furiously, people standing back from the heat of it. At least sixty feet beyond the blue car a man lay on his face on the grass of the center strip. The trooper and a man in T-shirt and jeans were taking people out of the brown car. Paul saw what they were taking out, and he took Joyce by the shoulders and turned her away. "Better not look," he said softly.

The crowd and confusion grew. While the more seriously injured were being loaded, the doctor cleansed Joyce's knee, wrapped it in gauze and quickly taped the gauze in place. "You both better stop in at the hospital in Blanchard for a checkup," the doctor said. "Just follow the signs once you get in the center of town."

One of the troopers had a portable battery-operated speaker. His voice was loud, harsh, metallic. "Get in your cars and clear the highway. Get in your cars and move along. You in the gray Buick. Move along. Go on. That's the way. Lady—you in the red slacks—there's nothing to see here. That's right. Just go back and get in your car. You kids gets off the highway. All right, you can get by there, mister. There's room. You're holding up the cars behind you. Let's get this show rolling, folks. Will the driver of the red Plymouth out in the field go to his vehicle, please."

Paul looked over and saw a tow truck in front of his car, a man fastening the cable on the front end. He hurried out with Joyce.

The man looked at them. "You own this? Unlock it and take it out of gear, please."

"Where are you taking it?"

"Ace Garage in Blanchard. You can ride in the car, or up in the truck with me. How'd you get way the hell out here?"

"I wouldn't want to try it twice," Paul said. "Can we ride in the truck?"

"Sure. We're ready to go."

The truck circled out of the field at what seemed to Paul to be a careless speed. The Plymouth, nose in the air, rocked and bounced behind them. The driver said, "Bunch of damn vultures. I swear there's ten tow trucks in this stretch of highway. We got three. We keep a radio turned on to the police band. If you think you got a chance, you jump in and go like hell. This brought everybody out. At least we got three jobs out of it. Scanlon got the truck. He got here first. That's the cream job. Brudderhoff didn't get a damn thing, and brother, that does my heart good.

"Two weeks ago I got a Mercury went into the ditch, rolls over twice. I mean, I really got there first. Hell, they were still taking a lady out of it. Like a damn fool I decide to swing around and get it from the other side. I'm backing the truck and when I look up there is that Brudderhoff with a hook already on the front X, grinning all over his damn face. The boss gave me hell. Brother, the next time I jump out of the truck, run my line out and slap a hook on the crate and *then* figure how I'm going to roll it. These vultures, they got no sense of ethics. It's not like we were that hungry for work. Hell, the shop is full up, but a truck like this, you got an investment. You don't get it back if the truck sits in your yard and the other boys go out and hook onto the business, do you?

"A month ago I guess it was there is this old Chev that busts down on a Sunday in heavy traffic. What turned out was, he threw a rod. Anyhow, he can't move it and Chuck, he's on the big wrecker we got, he gets there about the same time as the patrol car. Chuck was cruising. The boss says we cruise the big truck on Sunday. It's got a police radio in it. The Chev is in the middle lane and he can't get it over to the side of the road. Traffic is too fast. The troopers say hook on and get it out of there. The guy is crying. He's got a garage of his own, and he's in the other direction. Chuck says if he hooks on, he's got to bring it back to Blanchard. They practically have to hold the guy while Chuck hooks on. What a mess! Car full of screaming kids, and the guy's old lady giving Chuck a bad time. Chuck brings it in and then he won't let it down off the hook until he gets the fifteen bucks. Me, I'm too soft. I would hauled him off the road, dropped him and said the hell with it.

"Brother, you don't know what kind of a business this is. There used to be a sort of agreement about sharing the work, but it didn't last long. A thing like today, and you get all the vultures swarming in on it. This was a bad one. I took a look and come right out after your car. Chuck got the Cad and poor Sid got the burn job. Sid usually gets the messy ones. I don't know why. It just works out that way. Here we are, and you folks go right in there and talk to Ray. He's the service manager. It says so on his coveralls. Give him your name and he'll give you the poop on your crate here. It don't look too awful bad to me unless maybe the frame is out of line and then you got some expensive trouble."

Now they sat and waited to find out how expensive the trouble would be. They had found out about the truck driver. And the other deaths.

Joyce said, "Now you're frowning."

"Am I? I was thinking of that man Cherrik."

"And frowning?"

"It's a funny situation. I mean, what he did. Present from a stranger. Certainly he had a choice. He would have been shaken up a little and that was all. In a funny way I resent his making that choice so automatically. He gave us life and gave himself death. That simply. He didn't know us. There was no weighing of pro and con. Maybe it's the instinctiveness of it I resent. Or maybe I just resent facing the realization that there lived a man who could make that choice."

"Made that choice right after you said so firmly that people stink."

"Don't rub it in, girl. I'm trying to be frank. I'm trying to tell you everything in my head. I sense the presence of an obligation. See what I mean? Gift of life, so the obligation is to use it in a manner worthy of the giving. That's oppressive, don't you think? It makes your life something not quite your own. You have to be worthy of a gesture."

"Isn't gesture too little a word?"

"Yes. More than that. A choice. A . . . an instinctive way of thinking and reacting. I don't know. Maybe I think too much. Now I find myself thinking in terms of some sort of cosmic scales, with his death on one side and our life on the other. So that should we live meanly, do small things, hateful things, the scale will be out of balance. And that, of course, is a ridiculous and quasi-sentimental way to look at it."

She touched his hand, tilted her head to one side as she looked at him. "Is it? Why not accept it that way, Paul? A second choice. For us. Would it be . . . wrong or bad to be slightly mystic about it? Is there anything foolish about trying to live up to something?"

"N-no, I wouldn't say that exactly, but what he did was part of a chain of events that had nothing to do with us. It was the blue car that went out of control. I drove as well as I could."

"Why didn't the chain of events have anything to do with us? Remember lunch? It got pretty dreadful, didn't it?"

"Yes. I'm sorry about that."

"I don't mean for you to be sorry. While we were eating I saw a woman have dessert. Ice cream with fudge sauce. It looked heavenly. I decided I wanted some. Then we bickered and I lost my appetite. I decided not to have it. So we were at that precise place on the highway because we quarreled. Otherwise, we would have been about ready to pay the check."

"Wait a minute! We wouldn't be on this trip if things hadn't started to go sour."

"I know that. And, darling, I know we wouldn't be together at all if I hadn't changed jobs and gone to work with the insurance company, or if my father never met my mother, or if, or if, or if. Goodness, there are billions of ifs going all the way back to the dawn of time that put us finally right there, in front of that truck. But can you say there was absolutely no free will involved? Didn't we make *some* choices that put us in front of that truck?"

He thought it over. "Yes. Of course."

"So is it all right if I accept that . . . oppressive responsibility you mentioned? If I want to accept it?"

He smiled. "But it doesn't fit you. You would live up to it anyway."

"Oh, I do lots of hideous little things, and think of awful things."

"It fits me better than you. Look, be patient with me. I learned something today. There are still a thousand rough edges. But I'm going to try."

They looked into each other's eyes. He looked at his watch and saw that it was time and they went over to the garage. The mechanics had left. The service manager was sorting work orders. The garage was silent.

"Yes?"

"My name is Conklin. You told us to come back and . . ."

"Oh, sure. The Plymouth. Here's the bad news. You'll need a new front left fender, new grill and new radiator. And new springs and shocks in the front end, new steering arms, king pin, and a new left front wheel. The frame isn't sprung, and there's no rear end damage. It looks like about four hundred bucks. Have you got collision?"

"Hundred dollar deductible."

"Better wire your insurance company. And I see you got a personal injury, lady. There'll be death claims and total loss stuff floating around, but don't let them brush you off. This place will be crawling with adjusters tomorrow."

"How long will it take for our car?"

"If you want to authorize me to go ahead, I can maybe have it for you by noon Thursday. Will that be okay? I can't do any better."

"I guess it will have to be. Can you recommend a place to stay?"

"There's a lot of good motels. Try the Night Wind. There's a chance they're not full up yet. Here's the phone. It's in the book. They're about a half-mile east of here, on the right."

He handed Joyce the phone book. "You try while I get what we need out of the car."

The car was in back of the garage. The yard was fenced. The burned car was in a corner of the yard. The blue Cadillac was parked beside their car. The service manager came out back with him. "Isn't that Cad a mess though? Total loss. We can strip a few hundred bucks off it, but that's all. Can't get even that much out of the Olds."

"What will you do with them?"

"We'll make a bid. Then it's up to the insurance adjusters. If they think they can get more, they can move them out. Say, if you folks want a ride to the motel, I'll be through here in another five minutes."

"We'd appreciate it," Paul said.

When he went back in, carrying the two suitcases, Joyce said that the Night Wind was holding a double for them. After a short wait, the service manager dropped them off. Paul explained about the car and about wanting the room

for three nights to the woman behind the desk. The room
was large and attractive.

Paul sat on the bed and smoked a cigarette while Joyce
busied herself with unpacking, hanging their clothes up. He
leaned back on one elbow and watched the slim quick body
of his wife as she walked quickly back and forth, humming
to herself.

"Leg all right?" he asked.

"Doesn't hurt a bit, dear."

She had taken off the stained sandal and she looked at it
ruefully, and then bent her knee and looked back down over
her shoulder at the dark mark of blood caked on the sole of
her slim foot. She took off her blouse and went padding into
the bathroom in bra and skirt, closing the door behind her.
Paul, watching her, had felt the growth of a truly astonishing
desire for her, stronger, sharper, deeper than it had ever
been before. His hand shook as he lifted the cigarette to his
lips for a last drag before putting it out in the glass ashtray
on the night stand between the beds.

When she came out of the bathroom she gave him her
quick smile and went to the dressing table and sat there,
very straight, and began to brush her dark hair, looking at
herself gravely. With her arms high, her breasts, shiny in
white nylon, stood out sharply, lifting with the stroke of the
brush. The bra strap bit lightly into the velvet of her back.

"Joyce." His voice was rusty, arresting, and the after-
tone of it seemed to hang in the air of the quiet room. She
turned quickly, brush poised and still in the air, dark hair
falling about her face, soft to her bare shoulders. She looked
at him for a long moment of awareness, lips parting and face
changing. She laid the brush down on the glass top of the
dressing table with a tiny click of plastic against glass. She
stood up, facing him, her eyes downcast, and walked slowly
toward him stopping just out of his reach, as if this were, in
a sense, an offering.

She reached back and unhooked the bra, let it slide down
her arms and drop to the floor. She did not look directly at
him. Her breasts were firm, sharp, tipped with duskiness.
Still she did not look at him. She kept her eyes turned shyly
away as she stood there before him, offering warmth and
richness.

She advanced toward him. He was sitting on the edge of
the bed. He pulled her close, his arms around her. Her body
was cool, warming under his hands.

They were there together in the slow dusk, quickly and slowly, strongly and tenderly, with sureness, and awareness and recognition. They were there while the coming of night hushed the fast traffic sounds, and the trucks snored westward, and the lights, coming through the slots of the blinds, tracked across the ceiling and made small sparks in her wide, wide eyes.

Afterward they lay in that special quiet place of the shared cigarette, the slowing heart, the long deep sigh that would catch a bit, as with a memory of tears.

"They say it does this," he said. "Brush too close to the skirts of death. Then everything has a special high wild flavor, a special spice."

"Mmm," she said.

"You know, honey, I keep getting amused at myself. Subjection to pure corn. A moment of realization. Me! A big fat juicy moment of realization—you know—past life spinning before my eyes."

"Mmm."

"Now I know what that moment of realization is like. It's like this. My vision was diffused. Like looking at everything from several different angles at once, with the lenses all out of focus so that things overlapped and I couldn't see any single thing in clear outline. Then click. Something turned all the knurled knobs and the lenses were in focus and everything was bright and clear the way it should have been all along."

"Mmmm-hmmm."

"Like needing a change of glasses and not knowing it. Then getting the new pair and finding that trees are not green blobs, finding they have individual leaves."

He started to butt the cigarette and she caught his wrist and took a last drag.

"Gosh, I'm so hungry I could bark like a dog," she said.

He laughed softly. They got dressed and went out to eat.

chapter 12

DEVLIN Jamison was awakened in the very early morning by a starched nurse who took the opportunity presented by his first vague word to put the chill thermometer under his tongue. She took his wrist and stood, looking at her watch, moving her lips as she counted. She was a wide swarthy woman with an ugly good-tempered face. She dropped his wrist and walked to the window and looked out at the morning. After a time she returned to the bed, took the thermometer and took it toward the window to read it before shaking it down.

As wakefulness reached down through his body, Jamison became aware of a veritable symphony of aches and stiffnesses. Once upon a time he had fallen, with full pack and carbine, from a landing net into a Higgins boat. The awakening on the subsequent morning had been much like this one.

He looked down through a portal in his mind and saw the crash of the blue car, saw himself sailing through space. He closed the portal quickly. He did not want to think about it yet. The sedative had stuffed his head with cotton waste. It pressed dryly against the backs of his eyes and frayed into his throat.

Through another portal Gina lay waxen, banked with flowers. He closed that opening also.

"How do we feel this morning?" the nurse asked.

"I don't know about you. I feel like a hammered thumb —all over."

"The doctor will see you after breakfast," she said, and rustled out.

When she had gone he looked around at the room. It was a pleasant room. Through the window he could see elm leaves and an edge of morning meadow. He laboriously pushed the covers aside. He was in a short hospital gown. It took cursings and prayers and many low gasps of pain before he had both feet flat on the floor. One one side of his body where he was not bandaged, he was blue. His chest was taped, one finger splinted. He heaved himself to his feet. With each move, abused muscles creaked, rubbed dryly. He went over and looked out the window.

He could see an old house, a brown puppy, and a small girl on a yellow tricycle. A woman came out on the porch and shaded her eyes. The small girl turned the tricycle around and pedaled back around the corner of the house and the woman went inside.

He stood with feet planted, opened the portal in his mind and let the memories flood in. He remembered the thumping of the front end, the blowout and the loss of control. He squeezed his eyes shut and hit his fist lightly against the window frame. He wanted a hole to open and swallow him up without trace. He wanted to hide from the eyes of every man. He felt sick with regret—and shame. People had died because he had been too careless, too distracted to do anything about his car.

He was still at the window when the nurse came with the breakfast cart. She scolded him back into bed, helped him lift his sore legs onto the bed. He barely noticed her, so deep was his depression. He ate little.

Dr. Budischon arrived at nine. He checked Jamison over. "I guess you can get up any time. I understand they brought your luggage over last night. I'll have someone bring it here. The personal things we took out of your clothing are in the office. Your clothes were ruined."

"I remember that. Did you contact Mr. Seiver?"

"Yes. He said he'd be here today. He'll expect to find you here. You're perfectly welcome to stay, of course, until he arrives."

"Doctor, I'm . . . a little fuzzy on what happened to the other people involved. Could you tell me . . . how bad it was?"

"There were six killed, Mr. Jamison. And two others injured. The two injured are here. One of them is in the next room, in fact."

"Six," Jamison said softly. He kept his eyes shut while Budischon explained who they were, and the relationships.

After a while the doctor left. A nurse brought his bags in and told him that the bath was diagonally across the hall. She left him a big towel. It took Jamison a long time to get cleaned up, shaved and dressed. It was not only the difficulty of movement, but also the way he kept getting lost in thought.

He caught himself standing with necktie in hand and realized he had been standing there for a long time. The splinted finger made him awkward and slow.

When he was dressed he closed his bags and sat in the armchair by the window and waited.

Roger Seiver came into the room with another man at eleven-thirty. Roger was a big rawboned man with lank blond hair. He had a trick of emphasizing statements with a jerk of his head that threw the blond hair forward. He would immediately smooth it back with both hands. He had a loose mouth, tiny blue eyes, a honking adenoidal laugh. He was a party clown of wide repute, and an exceptionally clever lawyer.

He came right to Jamison's chair, big hand outstretched. "No, don't try to get up, fella. They told me out front you took quite a shaking up. Dev, I want you to meet Hal André. He's with the Claims Department of Fidelity Mutual."

André was a young-old man with a black brush cut, a hard brown simian face, enormous black eyebrows. He was smallish, and handled himself with the trimness of the ex-athlete. His hand, in Dev's, was small, hard and dry.

Roger Seiver took the straight chair and André closed the door and sat on the bed. Roger said, "Well, it looks like you had some trouble, fella."

"More than that."

"After I got the phone call I phoned the State Police here and got a briefing. Then I got hold of Bill. I remembered he handles your insurance. He phoned the home office and they sent Hal André down and he flew down with me this morning. We both want to get straightened away on how this thing happened."

André smiled and said, "Mr. Jamison, your liability policy, the personal liability amount is quarter-million, half-million. Bill Howard was quite correct in selling you that quantity. It isn't much more expensive than fifty, one hundred. You can understand how, in a situation like this, we try to get on the job as quickly as we can. Once you give me the information, I'll go out and try to obtain releases, offering cash settlements if it turns out that you could be considered in any way to blame. We've discovered that if we move fast on these things, we come out better. We don't like to have anything go to trial if we can help it."

"I'm to blame for the whole thing," Jamison said.

André shifted uneasily and glanced at Seiver. Roger said, "Let's not jump too fast, Dev."

"It's perfectly simple. I had a bad thump in the front end. I stopped but they couldn't do anything about it. They recommended a place. I thought it was alignment or balance. It must have been a broken casing, a blister on the right front tire. I was negligent. I kept running on it. It blew and I lost control and killed those people."

"Now wait a minute, Mr. Jamison," André said sharply. "Were you drinking?"

"No."

"Were you exceeding the speed limit?"

"Yes. A car was coming up behind me. I swung out and stepped on it to get by and get out of his way."

"How fast were you going?"

"Seventy, I'd say."

"Did you look at your speedometer while passing?"

"No, I didn't."

"You could have been going sixty then."

"I know I wasn't."

"But unless you looked at the speedometer, you can't be certain. I brought your file along, Mr. Jamison. Our records show that you have been insured with us for eight years. On your original application you stated that you had never had an accident with damages in excess of one hundred dollars. Is that correct?"

"Of course."

"What is your arrest record for traffic violations?"

"Twice. Once for passing a boulevard stop. The grass was so high I didn't see the stop sign. I just slowed down and then went on. That was in fifty-nine. I was stopped for speeding in sixty-one. In Colonial Heights, Virginia, outside of Petersburg. I was going thirty-eight in a thirty-five-mile zone."

"That's a notorious speed trap," André said. "The AAA has it marked. That sounds like a good record to me, Mr. Jamison. Now, based on something Mr. Seiver told me on the way over, I must ask you another question. At the time of the accident were you . . . emotionally upset?"

"I started on this . . . vacation because my nerves were bad. I lost my wife recently. I wouldn't say that affected my driving, Mr. André."

"Precisely how did you lose control?"

"When the tire blew it swerved the car to the right. There

was traffic in the center lane. I swerved the car back a little too far and hit a curbing that runs down either side of the center strip. Once I hit the curbing the car was out of control. It was my fault in not having something done about the thumping sound."

André took his time lighting a cigarette. "Forgive me for saying this, Mr. Jamison, but you seem to be reaching for trouble. You had a mechanical failure. Just as if your steering failed, or your brakes failed. It was out of your hands."

"But I had fair warning."

"You knew a tire was going to blow?"

"No. Of course not. I knew something was wrong with the car. I thought it was alignment."

"Have you thought of this? Maybe the thumping sound was due to faulty alignment. And the tire blowing was something else again."

"Do you think that's at all probable?"

André shrugged. "It could happen. And I would imagine that with the present condition of the car, it would be tough to prove it either way."

"What are you trying to prove anyway? I carry that much insurance to pay for anything I might do with the car. Now I've done it. The insurance is in force. I don't see what you're driving at."

Seiver said hastily, "You've got the wrong slant on this, Dev. Hal can't go around trying to pay out as much as possible. Hell, the insurance rates would go out of sight. He's got to cut the claims down as far as possible."

"I'm to blame for this mess. I accept responsibility. I don't approve of moving fast and bullying people into small settlements."

André flushed. "Jamison, I don't like the inference. We represent you. We'll settle all just claims without bitching. But we don't cheat anybody—and neither will we turn into a charitable organization. Get that straight. You are not going to put us in the bag by going around beating your chest and yelling, *'Mea culpa, mea culpa.'* Maybe it would give you a masochistic charge to do that, but we're not in business to give you a stage setting as a suffering hero."

"Get out of here!"

"Gentlemen!" Roger said, grinning uncomfortably. "Leave us settle down here. Nothing you can say, Dev, is going to stop Hal from investigating and handling any possible claims in the way he thinks best, in the way he's been trained."

Jamison looked at him. "All right. And nothing can stop me from accepting financial responsibility for these people over and above the amount of any settlement André might make."

"Now hold it!" Seiver said sharply. "I'm your attorney, boy. I wouldn't be happy about the legal aspects of that. If André got unconditional releases, payment in full of all claims, I don't know how a court would consider any additional and subsequent payments on your part. They might be considered as opening it up again."

"We'd be in the clear," André said. "There's a precedent on that."

Jamison stared at André. "You don't seem to realize that . . . well, take just one person. The Scholl girl. Her whole family is dead."

André smiled. "You're breaking my heart, Jamison. Two months ago a big policyholder got taken drunk and went down a one-way street the wrong way and smacked a bicycle. The kid is eleven, and permanently paralyzed from the waist down. The judgment was a hundred and eighty-seven thousand six hundred dollars. I was there when our doctors went over the kid. And I have one boy ten and a girl twelve. Don't try to break my heart, Jamison."

"And you tried your damnedest to make the judgment as small as possible."

"Naturally," André said. "That's my job. Mr. Seiver, this guy is a bleeding heart. I've got all I need. I'll check back with you." He walked out, his stride brisk, not looking back.

After long moments Seiver said, "You've got to look at it this way, Dev. Take that Scholl family. When they went out on the highway they accepted an implied risk. If they weren't willing to take that risk, they wouldn't own a car, or take it on a vacation. Mechanical failure can happen to anyone at any time in fast traffic. And it can kill people."

Jamison shook his head. "I can't look at it that way."

"You're all upset because it just happened yesterday. In a few days you'll get your perspective back, Dev. Good lord, let the insurance company handle it. That's why you carry so much, so they can take the load. From what you say, you'll come out of this clean as a pin. There isn't any possibility of a manslaughter charge against you."

"Dandy!"

"And let me tell you one thing, Dev. You're pretty well

set, financially. Gina's trust funds revert to you. If you start trying to pay off your conscience—and you have no cause for a bad conscience—by giving money to any of these people, they could get a shyster lawyer and milk you completely dry. I want you to know that."

"Right in the next room, Roger, there's a woman who may live and may die. If she lives, she may never be right. I did that, Roger. She was minding her own business."

Roger frowned. "A woman? The Scholl girl is your only concern. That's the only car you hit."

"But the other people were hurt *because* I hit that car."

"Oh, there's no legal responsibility there, Dev. The law says they got into the mess because they didn't have their cars under control. Hell, take those twenty-car crashes in the fog on the Jersey Turnpike. The lead car jams on his brakes. Then bang bang bang. Twenty cars. Every driver is responsible for the car he bangs into. Maybe the lead car caused it by stopping, but there's no legal claim against him because he didn't hit anything. He was hit. Good lord, if the lead car could be made legally and financially responsible for the entire amount of damage, nobody could afford insurance. The law says if you hit something, your car is out of control."

"You don't have the faintest idea of what I'm talking about, do you?"

Seiver looked away. "I don't think you do either, Dev. I think you're heading for a mess. I think you want to bleed. Maybe it has something to do with losing Gina. I wouldn't know. But let me tell you that this can be one hell of an expensive way to punish yourself. Now, if you can leave here, let's go get some lunch."

Frazier lay on his back on the lumpy bed of a six-dollar cabin, blowing smoke toward the ceiling. Before the new road had been put through, it was possible that the cabins had done a fair business. There were eight of them, arranged in a shallow semicircle behind a small greasy café. They were grimy white with green trim, steeply pitched roofs. The new highway came too close to them. He felt the thunder of the trucks in the bed springs. New pretentious motels had taken the cabin trade.

The cabin suited him. The owner had been more interested in cash in hand than in the absence of car and luggage. The torn coat had been wedged under the mud of a steep ditch.

He had walked to town, purchased cheap sport shirts, toilet articles, a cheap bright leather jacket. His mouth was still puffed. When in town he had located the Ace Garage. He had stood outside the fence and looked at the burned Olds. The trunk compartment had been jimmied open. It was a few inches ajar. He saw that the luggage was gone. The two tires were there. He rubbed his palms on the sides of his pants and went away.

An article in the morning edition of one of the city papers had complicated everything. He picked the paper up and read it again.

The head was, "STOLEN CAR BURNED IN CRASH."

State Police announced late yesterday that a green sedan which crashed and burned yesterday afternoon in the accident near Blanchard has been identified as being stolen three days ago in Mobile, Alabama. On the same day that the sedan was stolen in Mobile, Mobile city police recovered an abandoned car which had been stolen the day before in Chiefland, Florida. The presence of stolen Florida plates on the car which burned here has led police to suspect that the men in the car may have been the daring bandits who committed the high noon robbery of the Williston People's Bank in Williston, Florida, last Thursday, walking out with an estimated forty thousand dollars.

A man and a woman, as yet unidentified, died in the flaming vehicle and another man escaped serious injury. He was helped out of the car by a passing motorist and later, after refusing medical treatment, escaped from the scene of the accident. He is described as being about thirty years old, medium build, dark hair and eyes, wearing a gray sports jacket with a torn left sleeve. As a result of the accident he had a bruised mouth and the knuckles of his left hand were scraped. The description matches that of one of the men who robbed the Williston People's Bank. Two revolvers similar to those used in the robbery were found in the luggage compartment of the burned car. It is expected that experts will examine the ashes inside the car sometime today to determine if the bank loot was destroyed in the fire. Police say they believe the man to be in the area. The FBI is flying pictures of suspects here in hopes that those who saw the man at the scene of the accident can make identification.

Frazier grunted and threw the newspaper aside. It was getting entirely too warm in the area. It would be smart to make tracks. They might check all transient registrations. But the forty thousand was there, nearly in plain sight. One stinking wire fence. He remembered how Charlie had crabbed about stuffing the money in the tire. But it hadn't taken long, and were they stopped for a casual search, it was a good place. Damn it, it was still a good place. He decided the practical attitude was to stop thinking of it as forty thousand dollars. Just think of it as stealing a tire. It had gotten too warm to keep thinking on the basis of wandering in and buying it. Yet the fence was high, and there were a lot of street lights around. He felt bitter amusement. No great problem in cracking a bank, and stopped by the vast problem of stealing a tire from a car that was a total loss.

He got up restlessly and went to the cabin door and looked out through the screen. In another hour it would be time to eat lunch at the greasy spoon out front. Traffic blared and blasted by, swirling hot air across the parched ground in front of the cabins.

A girl sat on the single step of the cabin directly across the way. She was hefty but slim-waisted. She wore white shorts and a red halter. Her round heavy legs, exposed to the sun, gleamed with tanning lotion. She wore dark sunglasses and her dark hair was frosted over the temples. He recognized her as the girl who had served him breakfast that morning and dinner the night before. She had seemed willing to be friendly, and not overly bright. He looked at his watch, shrugged, and pushed out through the screen door. He put his hands in his pockets and sauntered over to where she sat.

"Hi," he said.

"Oh, hello there."

"Getting some sun?"

"Trying to get some tan, darn it. But you just watch. In five more minutes he'll be bellering out that back door and I'll have to change and go to work."

"You live right here?" he asked. She moved over on the step and he sat down beside her.

"If you can call it living. I got stranded here. How I let

him talk me into working for him, I'll never know. The tips, he says. The tips will pick up, he says. In that joint a dime is a big situation."

"I left you two bits."

She grinned at him. "Exception. I put it in my hope chest. My hope is I hope I get out of here. Say, my name is Donna. Donna Heywood."

He had no difficulty remembering the name he had registered under. "I'm Stan Kenton, just like the band leader."

"Hey! How about that! I bet you take an awful ride, having the same name."

"I get kidded some," he said.

"Got a cigarette? Thanks. Now how come you're stuck here?"

"I'm waiting for a job to start. Construction. I got here too early, so I have to hang around. I was down the road, but it was too expensive. So I moved out here."

"Al said you don't have any luggage."

"Oh, I checked that down in the bus station. I just brought a toothbrush out here. I didn't know if I could sleep, with its being so close to the road. So I didn't want to go lugging my stuff all over."

"Sure. That's smart. I didn't sleep worth a damn at first, but now I don't hear a thing. This crummy job is just temporary with me. Joey, she's my girl friend, and I, would you believe it, we started out from Brockton, Mass., way last January, headed for Las Vegas, and this is as far as I got. She's been out there a couple of months already. I got stuck on account of Miranda."

"Miranda?"

"My car, forgive me if I use the expression. She's sitting in a garage down in town until I can get her out of hock. She used to belong to both of us. We chipped in and bought her for the trip. Boy, did we ever take a reaming. It's a fifty-six Studebaker. It broke down last January right in Blanchard. There was no point in us both staying here. We flipped and I lost. I had to buy out her share. She went on by bus."

"Is it all fixed?"

"Oh, sure. And the bill is down to about thirty-five bucks. In about one month I ought to be on my way again. Joey's got a job lined up for me. Heck, I tried to sell Miranda but I had to take too big a loss. I guess I should have, way back in the beginning, but I've been hanging on this long, I might as well go the rest of the way."

He kept his voice level as he asked, "What garage is she in?"

"Oh, the biggest one in town. The Ace Garage."

"Is she parked out in the back?"

"I guess so. If she was in inside storage those buggers would be charging me for it."

He felt a good warmth in the pit of his stomach. Luck had looked bad. All of a sudden it had changed. All you had to do was wait, and luck flipped right over on the other side.

He looked at her in the intent way that he had learned was generally successful and said, "Honestly, Donna, I couldn't figure what a girl like you was doing in a joint like this. That's why I wandered over, just to find out."

Her brown eyes wavered and fell. "A great line, Stan."

"It's no line. I mean it. I knew it had to be some kind of crazy setup. I knew that as soon as I saw you last night. Hell, on construction work I roam all over the country. I can size up people. I see a lot of them. I knew you didn't fit in this place."

She smiled, pleased. "Well, like the man said, it was the only game in town. It isn't bad, really. The rent is for free. That's what usually eats up your pay, buying a roof."

"Isn't that the truth? You should see the slobby women they usually have in greasy spoons like this. Now take you. You got a cute figure and nice eyes and . . . well, you're just a darn good-looking girl." He looked at her earnestly.

"I think you've been in Blanchard too long."

"Maybe I have. There certainly isn't much to do, that's for sure. You know, I've been wondering whether I should just take off. This would be a long job, once it starts, and I can't see spending a year in this place."

"Haven't you got a wife or anything?"

He looked beyond her, making his face stern. "I had one once, Donna. I wouldn't want to talk about it."

She touched his arm quickly. "Gee, you poor guy. Some women can be awful tramps."

"You wouldn't be like that."

"No, I . . . say, what are we getting into here?" She laughed nervously.

"I was saying that maybe I wouldn't hang around."

"Where would you go?"

He looked at her until her eyes fell again. He said softly, "I might even try Las Vegas."

"Now back up, brother. Hold it. This is moving too fast for Donna."

"Well, why don't we talk it over?"

"What's there to talk over?"

"What time do you get off tonight? I can pick up some cold beer from the man and we can sit out here in front of your place and knock off the beer and count up our money and see if we can plan anything."

"Maybe you've got me wrong, mister. Maybe you think I'm something I'm not. Just because I work in a . . ."

He held his right hand up. "Hush now. I'm not thinking what you think I'm thinking. This would be a business deal."

"Oh, sure!"

"It would, I swear."

She studied him, then grinned. "Okay, Stan. I get off about ten. It won't hurt to talk, anyhow. And make that ale."

The man opened the back door of the café. "Donna! What the exact hell is holding you up?"

"Coming, coming!" she yelled back, and whispered, "What a jerk! I got to go in and change now." Five minutes later, as he stood in his doorway, he saw her walk toward the restaurant in her green seersucker uniform. She looked toward his cabin, smiled and waved. He waved back. She walked on, with a slightly exaggerated motion of her abundant hips.

Frazier stretched out on his bed again. He blew smoke at the ceiling. The plan was beginning to form. He'd tell her he had a few hundred bucks. He'd go down there with her and use thirty-five of his funds to pay the balance of the bill on the car. The rest wrote itself. "Honey, I better check this thing over. Give it a good going over. These boys will let me borrow tools. Why don't you go buy something pretty for the trip. It'll take a half-hour maybe. I'll pick you up over at the drugstore."

With a free half-hour in the yard, there would be the right moment. Put the tire in the Studebaker. He could tell her he bought it. Maybe it would be smart to actually leave town with her. Yes. That would be best. Protective coloration. She would wonder about his luggage. He'd think up something to tell her. He'd have to buy some kind of bag to hold the money. As soon as they got in the first big city, it would be no trick to walk off. Maybe, if he used the time and the beer right tonight, she'd be so damn happy and friendly he could get away with telling her practically anything. It sometimes worked that way. The blonde had been a lot betterlooking. He wondered, idly, what the blonde's last name had been.

chapter 13

BERNARD Krissel arrived in the city by train at two P.M. and caught a bus to Blanchard. He was a dark lean man with a narrow face, poor posture and nervous movements. Under his dark eyes the flesh was puckered and discolored, like tiny gray velvet draperies. In contrast to the frail, unwell look of the rest of him, his hands were huge and meaty, malformed by labor. But it was labor performed long ago. They were soft, carefully manicured. He wore a pale gray suit with a wide black mourning band on the sleeve. He carried a scuffed black briefcase. He wore a black Homburg. The turned-up brim made his face look thinner and weaker.

He sat near the front of the bus, by the window. A massive woman with a pink face sat on the aisle, exuding body warmth. Krissel gave her many quick furtive glances. He sniffed explosively time after time until at last she turned her big head slowly and stared at him out of small blue eyes.

"You have to forgive me, lady. I am all upset today. Maybe you heard of the terrible accident near Blanchard?"

"I heard something about it. Yeah."

"Now I got to go there on account of it was my family got killed." He sniffed again.

Her eyes sharpened and she licked her underlip. "You don't say!"

"That's right. My sister. Dead. My brother-in-law. Dead. My littlest niece. Dead. My other niece. At death's door." Each time he said "dead" he snapped the big white fingers on his right hand. "Happy people off on a vacation. And bang. Like that. Murdered in their happiness on the road, singing, laughing and suddenly it is over."

"Gee, that's terrible," the woman said.

"I got the phone call in my office yesterday. I thought it was some terrible joke. Believe me, it was like the world fell down. You have no idea. Death you always plan on. It happens to all of us. But so many!"

"Yeah."

113

"Bert was a hard-working man. He thought of nothing but his family. Their pleasure. Beautiful daughters he had. All his hopes and dreams."

"It sure is a terrible thing. Four years ago my cousin was on a trip out to Bakersfield where . . ."

"I was just sitting in my office and the phone rang. You have no idea. Alice said she would send me post cards. I never got married. They were my family. Those girls were like my babies. It was a criminal that killed them."

"Huh?"

"A way of speaking only. Anybody who kills them in their happiness is a criminal."

"I see what you mean."

"Bert almost went in business with me once. I begged him. I did everything but get down on my knees. But he wanted to stay in the mill. He liked the mill. He liked using his strength. He said he was not for offices. I have a wholesale business. Three salesmen."

"My cousin . . ."

"Now it becomes my responsibility. The oldest girl, if she lives. To make a home for her, educate her." He slapped the briefcase. "The copy of the will is in here. I have the legal say. It was like a joke when they made it out with the lawyer. What could happen? Well, it just goes to show."

"You never can tell," the woman said. She clutched her packages and started hitching her weight toward the edge of the seat. "Would you pull the cord, please? I get off here."

Krissel pulled the cord. She stood up after the bus stopped. She said, "Well, it's a terrible thing."

"Thank you for your sympathy," Krissel said loudly. She lumbered to the front of the bus and got off. As the bus started up Krissel looked down out of the window into her upturned blue eyes. A nice sympathetic woman. The two women in back of him were whispering. He caught the words "accident" and "brother." He sat up straighter and sniffed loudly again.

At the bus terminal in Blanchard he found that the hospital was nearly a mile away. He found a taxi. The newness of the hospital surprised him. He paid off the taxi with money from a deep brown purse.

To the girl inside he said, "I am Mr. Krissel, the uncle of the poor Scholl girl, please."

"Oh, yes, Mr. Krissel. Dr. Budischon will want to know you've arrived. Will you have a seat, please."

"I must insist on seeing my niece, young woman."

"Just have a seat, sir."

He remained standing. Dr. Budischon came briskly into the waiting room. "Would you step this way please, Mr. Krissel." He took him into a smaller waiting room.

"Has Suzie died?"

"No, Mr. Krissel. She was banged up but not seriously hurt. Today is Tuesday. I would say she can be released on Thursday. Certainly no later than Friday in any case. Naturally, she is in a state of emotional shock."

"Naturally."

"I don't believe she has completely comprehended the situation."

"So young! She couldn't . . ."

"I'm going to let you see her, but I must ask you not to be emotional. Be pleasant and affectionate. Reassure her. Tell her everything is going to be all right. Do you understand?"

"All right, Doctor? With her father and mother and her sister in their caskets? All right?"

"Mr. Krissel, get hold of yourself. If you go on like this I won't let you see her today."

Krissel drew a deep breath and let it out. "I will try to do what you say."

Dr. Budischon studied him for a few seconds. "All right, then. Come along with me."

Suzie Scholl's arm and hand throbbed. Her leg hurt when she moved it. When they had awakened her that morning, she had been confused. She hadn't known for a time where she was or what had happened. But, little by little, it had come back. She had found stark clear pictures in her mind of how they had looked. She hadn't wanted to talk to the nurse, or smile at her, or co-operate. She had just wanted to lie and look at the wall and try to figure it out.

Dead. It was a funny word. If you said it over and over in your head it didn't mean anything any more. A word that was a funny sound, like knocking on something. All of them dead.

She remembered how she had imagined her sister dead a lot of times. Connie would be very still, wearing white satin, her face cold and hard like artificial fruit, her lips smiling a little, her hands folded over the stem of a flower. She would be in the front room. Mother and Dad wouldn't be able to stand it. They would be back in the bedroom crying. And when people came to see Connie, she would let them in. She would wear black and no lipstick. She would talk in a whisper and keep her eyes down and lead them into the living room where they could look at her. The women would bring food to the back door. Cakes and casseroles, and everybody would whisper and the house would smell of flowers.

She remembered that by thinking of that hard enough she had sometimes been able to make herself cry. But she couldn't find tears now, because it wasn't like she had imagined it. That ugly thing she had seen couldn't be Connie.

Connie was dead and she couldn't find any meaning in it. Or in her mother and father being dead. She could think of them, just how they were, and close her eyes and see their faces and even hear them talk, but it didn't mean anything that they were dead. It was something that had happened. She knew she ought to feel grief. Terrible grief. It was awful when you thought about it. Four of them and just her left. It was like you would read in a book or see on one of those sad television things. It was easy to cry at the television. So it ought to be a lot easier to cry when it was real. The pain she felt ought to be nothing compared to grief. But the throb in her arm kept getting in the way of thinking about it.

Nothing would ever be the same again. She tracked that thought back through the mild jungles of her mind and found that she could not feel loss that things would never be the same again.

She was looking at the wall when she heard his voice. She turned and looked at him, standing there, black hat in one hand and briefcase in the other.

"Hello, Uncle Bernie," she said.

He stood for a moment, looking tragic, and then came toward her. "Suzie!" he said. "My little Suzie! Darling, are you in pain?"

"I hurt some. But it isn't bad, Uncle Bernie."

He sat beside the bed and held her good hand in both of his. His big white hands were cool and moist and unpleasant. "Everything is going to be all right, darling. I swear. Everything is going to be all right."

"That's a funny thing to say," she said, frowning.

"I'll take care of you, dear."

"They're all dead. I don't see how you can change that."

"Nobody can change that, dear. Nobody."

He looked at her and his dark eyes filled with tears. He

put his head down on her bed and began to cry. His black hair gleamed with the tonic he used. His shoulders shook. He had her hand imprisoned, his forehead touching her wrist. A tear fell like hot wax on the back of her hand. She felt a sticky embarrassment and tried to pull her hand free, but he held it tightly. He had always made her feel creepy. He had always kept trying to tickle her and fondle her, long after she had gotten too big. His eyes would shine in a funny way and he'd giggle.

"Poor Suzie," he cried, between sobs.

She didn't want it to happen again, not with him there. She had not felt the least bit like crying. But all of a sudden the tears came, a hot bursting, a tearing, a convulsive scalding spasm. She ripped her hand away from him. It suddenly seemed unbearable to her that he should be sharing her time of tears. She fought for control and obtained it long enough to yell, "Get out of here!"

Uncle Bernie raised a face so shocked she wished she could laugh. "Suzie darling!" he said.

"Go away, you old creep, God damn you!" she yelled.

It was Dr. Budischon who pulled him out of the room, holding onto his arm, Uncle Bernie looking back, Dr. Budischon's face red and angry. When he was gone she settled herself into tears. She curled herself into a nest of tears. It had started like a thunderstorm, and now it settled down to a long warm steady rain—tears without thought or reason. Just tears.

Bulky red-headed Lieutenant Thomas Fay shrugged and got up from his desk. "Okay, Mr. André. I see no reason why you shouldn't see it. Come on back."

They went back into a sunny room in the rear of the trooper station. There was a waist-high counter along one wall, and several items of laboratory equipment. Fay said apologetically, "We do some drunk tests, that sort of thing. Anything too technical, we send it up the line. Benny, let's see that section of tire off the Jamison car."

The man in shirt sleeves handed Fay a piece of tire casing two feet long, half a tire wide. Fay handed it to André. "It's a blowout all right. You can see that. The question was whether or not it blew when he hit the curbing. Now look right along here. See those threads, how discolored they are? That was an old break in the casing. That's where she blew. Now see how light-colored the threads are where the

blowout enlarged the break? That tire was broken so bad
that road dirt had a chance to get in on the threads. Hell,
the tube must have damn near been bulging out through the
break. Is that what you wanted to see?"

"That's a help," André said. "The policyholder is a little
. . . hysterical about this thing. You know, people killed.
He's sensitive. An architect. Artistic type. He wants to take
the whole blame."

Fay took the piece of rubber back and slapped it
against his palm. "This is what takes the blame, Mr. André."

"Does your investigation show that he was speeding?"

"No. He was passing legally."

"What's the paper work setup?"

"Oh, we turn a copy of our investigation over to the
deputy coroner of the county. He holds an inquest. This will
be death by misadventure. If our investigation showed somebody in the wrong, then after the inquest, the findings would
be turned over to the county attorney and he'd prosecute
for manslaughter."

"So from your end, Jamison is in the clear?"

"That's right."

André grinned ruefully. "I wish it were as simple from
my end. Civil actions are a hell of a lot trickier. Get this
thing to a jury and heaven only knows what they might
award, just because Jamison obviously has money and the
dead people just as obviously didn't. Thanks for co-operating, Lieutenant."

"Good luck to you."

"At least I'm not going to have to mess around with the
people who were in the Olds. How does that look, by the
way?"

Fay looked at his watch. "We're going to go down in a
while and give that car another going over. No money
burned inside it. The one that got out wouldn't have had it
in his pocket. Not forty thousand in medium bills. I can't
see it being stashed, or their mailing it to themselves. It's a
funny thing. And not up my alley. I got into this sideways.
I'm road patrol."

André thanked him again and went out to his rented
car. He took out his pocket notebook and looked up the
name and local address he had picked up from the Ace
Garage. Mr. and Mrs. Paul Conklin. Night Wind Motel. He
remembered passing the motel sign before he had gotten the
address. He drove down to the motel and found out that

the couple was in number ten. One carload of tourists was unloading into number eleven. He heard somebody laughing inside ten. He rapped on the edge of the screen door. A thin pretty girl in yellow denim shorts and a white blouse came to the door. André noticed that her right knee was bandaged.

"Yes?"

"They told me at the garage where to find you. My name is André. I'm with Fidelity Mutual Guarantee. I'd like to talk to you and your husband."

"Won't you come in?"

André went in, shook hands with Conklin. Conklin was lean and dark, with an angular saturnine face. "Who handles your insurance, Mr. Conklin?" he asked.

"Atlantic Casualty."

"Have you informed them of the accident?"

"I wired them last night, Mr. André."

"The accident report on file at the State Police office shows that you ran into the Jamison car, Mr. Conklin."

The room was quite still. They both looked at him. André returned the puzzled stare calmly.

"We hit that car, of course," Mrs. Conklin said. "But goodness! Paul did beautifully. That other car started bouncing around right in front of us."

"There's a distinct possibility that the Jamison car wouldn't have gone over into oncoming traffic if you hadn't hit it when it was out of control," André said.

The girl's face got pink. "That's the most utterly ridiculous . . ."

"Hush, Joyce," Conklin said. "Just what are you after André?"

"Proper assignment of liability. I can talk to the Atlantic adjuster, of course. Jamison's car is a total loss and he suffered bodily injury."

"And after you've scared hell out of both of us, you haul out a release form and give us one dollar and we sign gladly, and you tell us that Jamison can't come back on us because the dollar is an admission of his liability. So everybody is happy. Jamison must carry a big policy."

André had to smile. "You know the script. What are you after?"

"What do we want out of it? We got out with our lives. We'd have a tough time getting very much because we did hit him. I don't deny that. But we're not going to sign anything without the advice of my insurance company."

"Are you sure your wife isn't going to suddenly start to have a lot of trouble with that leg?"

"Are you suggesting that?"

André sighed. "This is a cynical business, Mr. Conklin. I'm not willing to admit Jamison's liability. But for the sake of getting this cleaned up, I'll offer you two hundred and fifty dollars for an unconditional release as of right now. I'm sure your company would advise you to accept. You understand that if Jamison had gotten his car back under control after you hit it, your liability would be quite clear."

"I'm afraid I don't want to sign anything today."

"It was a try," André said.

"Mr. André," the girl asked, "will the truck driver's family get something from Mr. Jamison's insurance?"

"I'm afraid not. The car and the truck were never closer than thirty feet from each other. As I understand it, the truck driver merely turned off the road. Lost his head or something. There's no liability there."

"He turned off to miss us. And we were in his way because Mr. Jamison lost control of his car."

"Too tenuous. I'm sure the trucking company has some sort of plan for things like that."

"It doesn't seem fair," Mrs. Conklin said.

"I have to be running along. I'll see you later."

Back at the hospital André found out from the girl that the Scholl girl's uncle had arrived. He was out walking around the grounds. He was upset. André set out to find him, saw him at a distance, leaning against a birch tree.

chapter 14

After lunch Devlin Jamison had Roger Seiver come with him while he found a place to stay. The cab driver recommended the Midlands Motel, but, lacking a car, Jamison preferred the conveniences of a hotel. The Hotel Blanchard was an aged brick cube, angular with windows. It was in the center of the old town, far from the main highway. It apparently existed mainly on the patronage of the men's service clubs, plus women's meetings and school dances. The lobby was tile and the main staircase marble.

Jamison's room had high ceilings, two gilt framed lithographs of Flemish masters, a two-ton bureau and an acre of bed. His golf clubs were an anachronism hastily concealed in the far reaches of a closet of garage dimensions.

Seiver, with hands in pockets, leaned against the bureau. "All I ask is just take it easy, Dev."

"I want to do what I can for those people."

"Okay. If you feel that way. But don't jump at it. Feel your way along. Hell, you're juicy meat for somebody hungry to get hold of. I'm supposed to protect your interest. Will you do this for me? If you decide you want to help, let me get a separate release form signed. In addition to the ones André will get if he can make out-of-court settlements."

"What would it say?"

"Something like this, only in attorney talk. I hereby state that I clearly understand that any monies I accept from Devlin Jamison after this date are to be construed as gifts to me and in no way do they imply any obligation on the part of Mr. Jamison to continue such gifts. Nor does my acceptance of said gifts infer any continuing liability as the result of accident on blah blah blah and so forth."

"Suppose I want to accept responsibility?"

"Suppose I want to jump out yon window?"

Jamison was silent for a long time. "They're going to let me see them this afternoon. Miss Aller and the Scholl girl. I'd like to get back."

"I've got to get back to my office, Dev. Promise me you won't do anything until you check with me."

Jamison sighed heavily. "You're damn persistent. Okay. I promise."

"Now you're using the old head!"

They shook hands in front of the hotel. When Jamison looked back out of the taxi window he saw Seiver standing there, hands on his hips, looking after the cab with an expression of veiled irritation.

As Jamison walked toward the front door of the hospital, he saw André sitting on a bench in the side yard talking earnestly with a stranger in a black hat.

It was the neurologist, a tall, young-faced, gray-haired man named Dilby, who took Jamison in to see Kathryn Aller. Dr. Dilby had a strong enthusiastic voice. The polished lenses of his glasses reflected the lights from the windows. It was obvious that he took a special pride and interest in the motionless figure of Kathryn Aller.

Her face shocked Jamison. The purple eye, puffed shut, looked less than human. Her skin had a saffron tinge against the white of the head bandage. Some tangled dark blonde hair protruded from the top of the bandage that encircled her head. She breathed heavily through her mouth. She lay straight in the bed, her arms at her sides, straight on her back with her legs close together, the coverings molded to the long classic lines of her body. The bed looked unused.

"Yes, I think it's a safe guess to say that we won't find any permanent damage here, Mr. Jamison. Now watch this."

He brushed her closed eyelid with his fingertip. The woman squinted her eye. The reflex ceased as soon as he took his finger away, occurred again when he touched her eye again. "See?" Dilby said proudly. He bent over and put his lips close to her ear. "Kathryn! Kathryn!" The steady breathing changed. "Kathryn! Open your mouth, Kathryn!" The parted lips opened wider. Dilby straightened up and the slack mouth changed to its original position and the breathing continued.

"This is just an impairment of consciousness, Mr. Jamison. It's not as deep as it was when they brought her in. You saw how I could get some response. That's a good sign."

"Will she continue to come out of it?"

"Oh, I imagine so. Some of them come out of it all at once. Others come back slowly. She may go through a period when she'll do just about anything you tell her, but not know she's doing it. And there may be some traumatic amnesia."

"Could that last long?"

"I've personally treated a case where it lasted seven years. But that was unusual of course. Quite unusual. I anticipate a normal improvement. In three weeks' time she could be herself again."

"She could be."

"In three weeks or three months, returning slowly or all at once. These cases differ. A very mild case would be, for example, the football player in the shower room who suddenly starts asking how the game came out. He played, but after being hit, he played automatically. The worst case is the coma that grows deeper and deeper until the patient just . . . stops. Then autopsy shows us considerable brain damage, tiny hemorrhages. She doubtless has small brain hemorrhages, but from the way she reacts, I would judge that the pinpoint clots are being reabsorbed. I'm afraid I have to get back to my appointments."

"Would it be all right if I stayed here a little while?"

"Well . . . I guess so. If you want to. But . . ."

"Is she aware of what goes on around her?"

"Oh, I doubt that very much. She's just this much this side of complete unconsciousness." The doctor held up thumb and finger, a millimeter apart. He looked uncertainly at Jamison, hesitated in the doorway, then nodded and hurried off.

Jamison picked up a chair and put it close to the bed. He sat and looked at her still face, listened to her breathing.

After a time he was able to look at her face without seeing merely the bruise and the bandage. He saw, almost with astonishment, that the configuration of her face was good, a noble height of brow, a Grecian symmetry. She reminded him of someone he had seen long, long ago. It took him a long time to remember, and then it came to him. A movie actress named Ann Harding.

She breathed through her mouth and her lips were dry and cracked. Her breath was slightly unpleasant. Sitting there, looking at her, he remembered the times he had watched Gina's sleeping face. In sleep a person went away from you. Their lips became strange. Under the bone of brow moved the unknown thoughts and the far strange images. Yet, even in sleep, Gina's face had been his—marked by him. Known to him. He remembered the times of awakening her with a kiss, feeling the slackness, the small start of surprise, and the welling response. Gina's sleep had been of her choosing, and she had welcomed his awakening of her.

This woman was lost and far in a place not of her choosing. He had caused this silence, this cracked mouth, this saffron texture of her skin. The angry bruise lay against the flesh and, far below, she wandered in strange dreams. This face was not dear. This was a mouth which had been used by others. Smudged lids covered eyes he had never seen, eyes that had never looked on him.

Yet, watching her there in the silence, hearing the small distant noises of the hospital, he felt an unexpected closeness, a warmth toward her. She lay helpless because of him. He felt sorrow and pity—and a certain awe. He sensed the great will of the organism to survive. It would go on breathing, and the mind would heal itself and lift itself up out of blackness until a time when the eyes would open and look around with confusion, and the brain would demand to know what had happened. What caused this? Why am I here?

There was a hypnotic quality in the cadence of her breathing. He realized that his imagination was carrying him into strange, perhaps unhealthy regions. He resisted the imagery, and then surrendered himself to it. Gina, badly hurt, had died. This woman, badly hurt, lived. Death, as a force, had taken one and now reluctantly surrendered another. In the body sense the two women were more alike than unlike—a clear similarity of womanness. Breasts and pain and gentle mouth. Could it be that in some wild symbolic way this woman was given him, that this was, in truth, the dedication he had sought?

He was repelled at once by the thought of disloyalty to Gina. It was absurd to think for a moment that in this stranger there was an essence of Gina. There could be no transmigration. This woman could not descend so deeply into a coma like death that she could come back with any trace or tinge of Gina within her.

Jamison knew that he was imagining too much about her by merely watching her unconscious face. Affinities were too rare for that. Unconscious, she could be anything he wished her to be. But, very probably, when the brain regained control, it would be a vapid, stereotyped, irritating mind. One of those minds which, under the iron stamp of convention, were turned out like so many cookies—a mind and a set of reactions desolately predictable, emitting endless clichés in a flat, prim, nasal voice. The body alone would be unique and believable, but the growth of the mind would have ceased at seventeen.

He told himself that, yet could not believe it. He put his lips close to her ear as Dilby had done. "Kathryn!" he said. "Kathryn!" The regular tempo of the breathing changed —evidence of the mind fighting for light.

He spoke her name again, more sharply, and as she exhaled she vocalized a small rusty sound: "Ehhh." It was such a small tired sound. Such a desperate hidden cry. It touched his heart. He wanted her to know that she was watched over. He wanted her to know the comfort of touch. He thought that would reach her. He glanced guiltily at the open door, and then he turned the corner of the covering back, found her hand, took her arm gently out from under the covers and placed it so that he could hold her hand. Her hand was hot and dry. The fingers were slim, tapering, with tiny pads of callus on the tips of the fingers. He found her pulse with his fingertips. Her heartbeat was a slow strong vital impact.

Holding her hand, he spoke her name again. The second time he said it her fingers flexed against his. He sat there holding her hand for a long time. She made that sound again. She closed her mouth, swallowed, breathed through her nose for a time. Then the lips sagged open as they had been before.

The nurse rustled into the room. Jamison released her hand hastily and stood up. The nurse glanced at the exposed hand and at Jamison. She set her apparatus down and neatly tucked the arm back under the covering.

"I have to give her an intravenous feeding now, sir."

He left the room.

André sat beside Krissel on the bench in the May sunshine. Krissel refolded a legal paper and put it in his briefcase. "You see, Mr. André, it is all legal. I am the guardian, the executor. I can act in this matter."

"Subject to the later approval of the probate court."

"That I will worry about. I can act. But you? Perhaps you have to go running to get permission?"

"I'm not a regional adjuster, Mr. Krissel. I can make decisions."

"Now let us talk about this poor child."

"On her bed of pain."

"Mr. André, I do not like that kind of talk."

"It is the kind of talk you have been using for the last twenty minutes. I'm willing to talk about her. But let's accept the fact that it's a tragic thing and you're grieving about it, and go on from there."

"Mr. André, since we must have a starting point, obviously, it will be my intention to bring suit in her name for a death payment of twenty-five thousand each for her mother, her father and her sister, and an additional seventy-five thousand for the care, maintenance and education she would have gotten from her family, plus, of course, all medical expenses and loss of property and so on."

"That's quite a starting point."

"I do not think the child should be too greedy. It makes a bad impression."

"And lawyer's fees eat up a lot."

Krissel shrugged. "But sometimes a jury will even award a judgment in excess of the amount asked for."

"Rarely."

"It can happen."

"Let's take a look at Mr. Jamison. Good driving record. Not a drinker. No accidents. A tire blew. He'd go on the stand. He'd make a damn fine impression too. Prominent architect. Nice guy. We'd introduce the police investigation in evidence. That investigation of course shows that Scholl's speed was estimated by witnesses as from seventy to eighty-five miles an hour."

"Neither of us are attorneys, Mr. André. I can only see this. I can see a happy family going on vacation. A worker driving his car on which he is making monthly payments. They have saved and planned. Who smashes their lives? A man going on a vacation. In a rich convertible, with golf clubs even. Top down, getting a nice tan. A big man. Successful. And what happens to him? A little shaking up. The child's life is ruined. What is it to him? He has insurance. He can buy a new car. The insurance company has lots of money. Enough to give this poor child the things in life that were taken away from her. Nothing can replace what she lost, of course."

"That's right. Let's see what she lost. She's seventeen. I don't think she would be going to college. But let's give her two years of business school. That's three more years of education. Then she would get married. I'm just thinking out loud. Let's say five thousand a year for the three years she'd be on her family's hands. And another five for incidentals. I think twenty thousand would be fair if, for example, Jamison had been drunk and going a hundred miles an hour and Scholl was stopped for a light. But we've got a different situation here."

"My dear Mr. André, you have a sense of humor that kills me. No matter how you dress it up, my brother-in-law was on his own side of the highway, and Mr. Jamison came across onto the wrong side and hit them and killed them. So if he was going eighty or two hundred, the jury is people. They think of themselves. They say what happens to me, to my loved ones, if somebody jumps over on my side of the road and smashes me?"

"And, my dear Mr. Krissel, the jurors will also wonder if they could get a whopping judgment against them just for having a blowout, a mechanical failure. Anyway, Jamison doesn't have the kind of insurance in the amount you're talking about."

"So he has other property. The insurance pays up to the limit and Jamison pays the rest."

"I'll grant you that jurors can get emotional, Mr. Krissel."

"Of course! And she is a pretty girl. And smart. I think she would cry if she had to testify. And the cast on her arm, it will not be off for a long, long time. Such a big cast."

"Mr. Krissel, we're both trying to do the right thing by your niece. I admire you for your . . . protection of her interests in this matter. We prefer to make out-of-court settlements whenever fair and possible. I'll tell you what I'll do. I'll double my estimate. I'll recommend a settlement in the amount of forty thousand dollars."

Krissel shook his head sadly. "No, Mr. André. No indeed. I could not shave this face in the mirror every morning if I permitted such a travesty. I would not be living up to my duties as uncle and guardian for the poor child."

"I think that as an evidence of good faith, you should revise your figures downward. I revised mine upward."

"That is a hard thing, to make bargains which concern the future of Suzie. I am reluctant. I will go this far only, Mr. André. One hundred and twenty-five thousand."

André leaned back and lighted a cigarette. "Let me see now. With that money you could give Suzie a good home. You'd have to buy one, of course. In a nice neighborhood. And you could give her the benefits of travel. You would go along as her guardian, naturally."

"It would take her mind off her sorrow," Krissel said.

"I think you better sue, Mr. Krissel."

"Of course the suit would be in the amount I originally mentioned."

"Of course."

"I had hoped we would reach a meeting of the minds, Mr. André. Court costs will take money that should go to Suzie."

"We have our own legal staff."

"Forgive me for saying this, Mr. André, but are you using good judgment? As you said, juries are unpredictable."

André smiled sadly. "We'll just have to take our chances, I guess. Sometimes it works out that way. But believe me, we will be fair. Should the judgment go against us, we shall ask the permission of the court to set the total amount of the judgment up as a trust fund in Suzie's name, to provide ample income for her education, with the amount remaining in the fund to revert to her when she reaches her majority. They generally go along with us on such arrangements where a minor is concerned. It keeps relatives from dissipating the funds through faulty judgment."

Krissel looked out across the green lawn. The two men sat side by side in silence. Krissel said, "I am her uncle. I am her guardian. My judgment would be good."

"Of course. You can advise her as to how to spend the income from the trust fund. Say a hundred dollars a week until she is twenty-one. She'll need your advice, I'm sure."

"But you would prefer to make a settlement?"

"A reasonable one."

"That would not be a trust fund?"

"Not with the confidence I have in you, Mr. Krissel."

"Perhaps our minds could meet on one hundred thousand."

"No, Mr. Krissel."

"No?"

"No."

"Then do you know where they could meet, maybe?"

"At fifty thousand, Mr. Krissel. That is the top offer. The final offer. I can have the papers ready for your signature tomorrow."

"Seventy-five thousand. Remember what she has lost."

"No, Mr. Krissel."

"Since we still do not have a meeting of the minds, maybe we could be fair with each other and split the difference."

André bit his lip. "I've gone too far offering fifty."

"Seventy."

"Mr. Krissel, I am going to lean way over backward. I'll

probably be criticized for it. I will offer a flat sixty, and we will not pay any additional expenses. The check will be here the day after tomorrow."

Krissel waited a long time. "I understand your position. It is a hard thing. I cannot take a chance on what a jury might do with the future of the poor child. I guess that is it, sir." He held his hand out.

André hesitated and took it. He stood up. "I'll get to work on the papers."

chapter 15

IN the late afternoon they told her that the man who had been driving the blue car wanted to see her. During the afternoon she had drifted warm on a sea of tears, suspended, misted. A tide of tears, that had ebbed and left her back in the world, drowsy, sated.

"Why?" she asked.

"You don't have to see him if you don't want to."

"I guess I'd just as soon. But why does he want to see me?"

"I really don't know, dear."

The man came in. Suzie decided at once that he acted sort of cute and shy. He was a big man. Old. In his thirties, maybe. His face had a tough look, but his eyes and his mouth weren't tough at all. Soft. He sat on the chair beside the bed and then turned and just looked at the nurse. She stood and stared back and then turned suddenly and left the room. You could kind of feel the strength of him, the way he made her leave.

"I'm Devlin Jamison, Susan," he said. His voice was deep and soft. Furry, sort of. It seemed to go right through her and echo in her chest.

"I'm glad to know you," she said, and her voice sounded meek and little. She looked at the bandage on the side of his face and his ear, and the funny thing on his hand. She tried to smile. "They got us both all bandaged up."

"Susan, I don't know how to say this. It's futile to say that I'm sorry. I just . . . would give anything to take back what happened."

He seemed to feel just awful. "That's all right," she said.

He gave her an odd look. "It's hardly all right. I don't believe you know what you're saying."

"Yes I do. I mean I feel terrible. But I'm not a little kid any more. It happened, Mr. Jamison. Things like that do happen. I mean you've got to figure that an awful thing like that *can* happen. That doesn't mean you've got to go around blaming yourself."

"It could have been prevented. I could have prevented it."

"Gosh, how?"

"I had a bad tire and I knew it. I could have had it changed."

He looked so acutely miserable she didn't feel shy of him any more. He was like a little boy. He even reminded her —just a little bit—of Barney when he'd done something wrong and felt bad about it and wanted to be forgiven.

"Mr. Jamison," she said firmly, "my father was a terrible driver. Honest. He was going eighty, I bet. He'd always get so mad when he was driving. He was always getting speeding tickets, and he cracked up three cars. I bet a good driver could have kept from hitting you. He had a terrible time getting insurance. He had to pay awful rates. He was all the time crabbing about it."

She watched his face carefully and saw some of the strain disappear from it. He looked beyond her at the wall. This could come out like the dreams, she thought. Like the movies. The real sad kind, but where it came out all right in the end. The accident had killed her whole family, and that tragic thing threw them together. He'd look on her as just a little kid, but one day he would look at her again and see that she was a woman.

She saw the gold band on his finger. Dreams tottered. She said, "Was your wife hurt too?"

"What? Oh, no she wasn't, Susan. She died not long ago."

"You must be pretty lonesome, Mr. Jamison." He'll have a big house. I could get well there. I could cook and clean and do the marketing. He'll come home from work and I'll have a drink made the way he likes it, and there'll be candles on the table, in a patio. I'll wear my hair up and look older. Neither of us have anybody left.

"I guess I am, Susan. I wanted to see you because I want to tell you something. I understand your uncle is here."

"Uncle Bernie. He's my mother's brother."

"He'll probably be dealing with my insurance company. I don't know what kind of a settlement will be made. It may go to court. I don't know. I want you to listen to this closely, Susan, and understand. From now on, I want to help you. I don't mean just right now. I mean until you're grown up. When you're in any kind of trouble, or need anything, I want you to come to me, to get in touch with me. I guess I could have had a daughter almost your age. I have no children. I want you to let me be sort of a . . . substitute father." He smiled at her.

The smile made Suzie feel breathless. It twisted her heart. "I . . . I don't want to put you out any."

"It will make me feel a lot better."

"I guess, in that case . . ."

"We can start right now, Susan. Is there anything I can do for you now? Anything you want?"

She bit her lip and looked at him warily. She didn't want to try to move too fast. But this might be the very best chance. "There's one thing. It's kind of hard to say."

"Yes?"

"Well, it's Uncle Bernie. I guess he'll be taking care of me. I guess it looks like I would have to live with him. I'm scared about that."

"What do you mean?"

"Well, he's creepy. You know what I mean?"

"I don't think I do."

"I don't think a young girl ought to live alone with him. He hasn't got any family. Even if he is my uncle, I don't think a young girl ought to live with him. You know what I mean?"

"I think I know what you're trying to say, but are you sure?"

"Sure I'm sure. The way he looks at me. And when he'd come to our house he was always kissing me. You know, it was supposed to be like an uncle, but it wasn't."

Mr. Jamison looked so shocked and disconcerted that Susan wanted to giggle. She kept her face straight. After a while he said, grimly, "I think I have a solution to that, Susan. Yes, I think I have the answer to that. I think I'll have a little chat with Uncle Bernie."

"Don't make him mad. He's got a terrible temper."

"I won't make him mad."

"I'll be awful grateful to you if you could . . . fix it."

"I'm glad you told me this, Susan." He took her hand. She squeezed his tightly and glowed at him. He released her hand hastily. "I better see if I can find him."

They told him at the desk that Mr. Krissel was also stopping at the Hotel Blanchard. Jamison got the room number and phoned upstairs. Krissel told him to come right up.

Krissel's room was a duplicate of Jamison's. They shook hands and Krissel said, "I'm so glad you came to see me,

Mr. Jamison. That poor child on her bed of pain. A tragic thing. It must weigh heavy on your conscience. I would hate to have such a thing on my conscience, sir."

Jamison repressed his immediate annoyance. "I'm sorry about it, of course."

"Now I must care for the child. She has no one else. It will be hard for me, Mr. Jamison. I agreed to a figure with Mr. André. Now I feel I was too hasty. He took advantage of my grief. I was not thinking clearly. All I could think of was I did not want to have the poor child have to appear in court. In court the attorneys would crucify her. So I have agreed to a small figure."

"May I ask how much?"

"Sixty thousand dollars, sir. Said quickly it sounds large. But when it must be spread over the years of her education, it is small indeed. A home must be provided for her. I live in a very tiny apartment by myself. It would not be suitable, of course. She must have advantages, a nice address, nice friends. I am a poor man. I will do all I can, of course. But . . . who can ever compensate her for the loss of her happy home life, her little sister, a mother's loving care, a father's pride and devotion?"

"I came here to talk to you about her future, Mr. Krissel."

"So?" The man's voice was quick with interest.

"I would like to be permitted to help."

"Financial help over and above the settlement?"

"Yes."

"That is very generous of you. Very, very generous. Though I have my pride, sir, it is good to know that I will be able to call on you for assistance throughout the years."

"That isn't exactly what I had in mind."

"Mr. Jamison, before we start planning for the poor child, I do not wish to sound too businesslike, but after all I am a businessman. If you could make out a small personal check payable to the child—a token check—then we can proceed to discuss the extent of the help you will give her."

"Before I give her any help whatsoever, I am going to have my attorney draw up an agreement for your signature, Mr. Krissel. He has already advised me about that."

Krissel sighed. "A sensible precaution," he said. "An unscrupulous party might take advantage of your generosity."

"Exactly. And in addition I want you to agree to allow me to make the decisions regarding her education."

"That is most unusual."

"Without that agreement there will be no financial help."

"If I should agree, what would you recommend?"

"A good camp this summer. A good private school until she completes her secondary school education. And then one of the better woman's colleges. I will give you no cash directly. I will pay all of the tuition and school and camp expenses involved. That will leave the cash settlement relatively intact. You will not have to provide a home for her. It will take the . . . heavy responsibility off your hands, Mr. Krissel."

Krissel shook his head sadly. "I am sorry. She is too young. She needs the comfort of a home. Later, maybe."

"Now or not at all."

"That sounds like an ultimatum, Mr. Jamison. I do not like that."

Jamison smiled. "It is an ultimatum. As executor and as legal guardian you are responsible to the courts. I am going to tell Susan about this offer. I believe that you are going to find it necessary to explain why you refuse to accept it."

"Susan will listen to me, sir."

"Susan told me an hour ago that she will not listen to you."

Krissel's face got very white. "What right have you to go to that poor child and turn her against me?"

"I understand that the court can take over the guardianship of a minor, and appoint someone else, if it appears that the responsibilities are not being carried out."

"You threaten me, Mr. Jamison."

Jamison thought a moment, then smiled again. "Yes, I guess I do." He got up and went toward the door. As he opened it, Krissel said, quickly, "I am upset. Give me a chance to think it over. Maybe your plan is best. I don't know."

Jamison went out into the corridor and closed the door. He knew that Krissel would accept. It made him feel good. He thought that it would be quite interesting to watch Suzie grow up. At seventeen she certainly was a rather blatantly sexy little wench. A different environment would refine and subdue that sexuality. She might turn into a thoroughly exciting woman, provided she accepted the program he had conceived. He quickened his step. He would return to the hospital and explain the program to her and impress upon her, somehow, how important it was for her to follow through, and not run off to get married too quickly. He hoped her mind would be good enough.

He had a vision of himself in some distant year, driving to a very good girls' school, picking up a new Susan Scholl, a young lady of charm and assurance, tastefully dressed, and driving her into, say Boston, for dinner and the theater.

The vision was so clear that he became amused at himself and then quite suddenly ashamed. The girl had been orphaned in an excessively brutal manner, and he was using that as a basis for egocentric dreams. Carry such nonsense far enough and it would degenerate into a Pygmalion script, with Devlin Jamison superintending the development and education of the young lady until she was at last of fine enough fiber to become his wife. When she was twenty, he would be thirty-seven. He wrenched his mind away from that, wondering if he were going slightly mad. Of the two, Kathryn Aller was by far the more likely Galatea.

"Would you hold the line for a moment and I will see if Mr. Houde will speak with you, Mr. Lanney."

"Make it fast, sister. I'm paying for this and I'm on a toy-sized expense account."

"Mr. Houde, Mr. Lanney, phoning from Blanchard, is on the line."

"Hello? Houde speaking."

"Mr. Houde, did you have a girl named Kathryn Aller working for you?"

"Yes! Why? Are you thinking of employing her? I gave her a letter of recommendation that . . ."

"It isn't that, Mr. Houde. She's been in an accident."

"What? Where? Is she hurt? Who are you, anyway?"

"Now don't get excited, Mr. Houde. I'm a newspaper reporter. The police have been trying to get a line on the next of kin. I thought I'd try her ex-boss."

"She's dead!"

"Look, I can tell you quicker if you stop butting in, mister. She got a good knock on the head. She's unconscious. There's no fracture. It may take quite a while before she comes out of it. Now who has she got that the police should get in touch with? That's what I want to know. . . . Have we been cut off?"

"No. I'm still here, Mr. Lanney. She hasn't got anyone. She had an aunt in Philadelphia, but she died a few years ago. She hasn't got a soul."

"That's pretty rugged."

"Yes, I guess it is."

"You sounded pretty upset. I just wondered if you had any personal interest."

"I don't think I know what you mean. She was my private secretary for some years. Very capable girl. Naturally I'm upset about it."

"She have a boy friend?"

"I don't know of any. I . . . never knew much about her life outside the office, frankly."

"Well, thanks."

"You're entirely welcome, Mr. Lanney. Sorry I can't be of more help. If you see her after she recovers consciousness, please tell her that I . . . I'm concerned about her, and would appreciate hearing from her."

"I'll do that."

Lanney hung up. Bowers, sitting on the corner of Lanney's desk, raised one eyebrow. Lanney shook his head. "No dice. The way he sounded, I'd guess they maybe kept late hours in that office. But nothing you could prove. That guy is cute. And Aller hasn't got anybody in the world who cares whether she lives or dies. Not a bad-looking dish either. What do you want me to do?"

"I guess it's dead then. I'll hang onto it. If she's still out like a light a week from today, I'll give it to Helen and let her squeeze a few tears for the Sunday edition. You got any ideas on any of the rest of them—I mean outside of the hot car angle?"

Lanney shook his head. "Not a thing, Billy. All the rest of it is routine."

"By the way, they got an identification on that guy who ran out."

"Hey! Is that right?"

"They had that Dr. Prace looking at mug shots. The guy he identified had used the same M.O. and there was a pick-up out on him for parole violation. Guy named Frazier, from Boston."

"We running it?"

"No. Nobody is. They think he may still be around Blanchard someplace. Why, I wouldn't know. So we're what they call co-operating."

"What are we running to keep it alive?"

"The girl that got burned. Identification. Here's what the county coroner's office gave out. A blonde five feet seven, about a hundred and thirty pounds, about twenty-five. One crooked front tooth. Gold wedding ring in her purse with the initials L.C.A. and F.X.M. engraved on the inside of the ring."

"That ought to turn her up."

"And we're running a map, with an X where the first car was stolen, and one where the bank was robbed, and another where they got the car that was cracked up. Dusty made a dotted line along the probable route up to the final X where they cracked up. Chances are the girl came from somewhere along that route."

"Or they took her south with them."

"Not likely. No clothes. They think she was a pickup. Probably some roadside joint they stopped at. Maybe she got a look at some of the money."

"So where is the money?"

"Good question."

The three men from the Federal Bureau of Investigation finished counting the money. One of them packed it neatly in a cardboard box, wrapped the box in brown paper and heavy twine. He wrote the figure $38,770 on the brown paper and initialed it. The man from Washington initialed it too.

They were in an office in the county courthouse. The sheriff cleared his throat and they all looked at him. "I can let you have the lend of some real good boys."

"Thanks. We've got it pretty well covered."

"Is Tommy Fay going to be helping you fellows?"

"Who is Tommy Fay?"

"That State Police lieutenant. The one found the money."

"Oh, the redhead. No. The SAC in the city has released enough agents to me so that we can handle it adequately, thanks. Now if you'd excuse us . . ."

The sheriff heaved a sigh and left the office.

When he was gone the three men pulled their chairs closer together. The man from Washington unrolled the scale drawing of the Ace Garage and surrounding area. He made little dots with the point of a very sharp pencil.

"The cars are here, here and here. The radio is in this office here. The man stationed in this office is the key to the whole thing. Williams, you'll relieve him at seven this evening. If Frazier makes a try at night, these spots over here will floodlight the whole yard. You've got the control switch for those spots in the office. And with the night glasses you can keep a very close watch on that car. Harrington, you relieve Williams at eight in the morning. If he makes his try during daylight, during working hours, don't depend too much on the two men we have planted in the garage. Just alert the cars. The owners and the service manager are the only ones in on this. I want the area to look normal.

"Frazier won't know the money is gone out of that tire. He won't know he's been identified. I'm banking on his making a try. Logical that he should. And you'll have the rifle in the office if he tries the fence. When that loud speaker blasts loose, he will probably freeze. He may try the fence, but I doubt it. Set now?"

The two men nodded.

"If a trap smells like a trap, it isn't any damn good," the man from Washington said.

chapter 16

WHEN Frazier left Donna Heywood's cabin, he stopped half-way across the baked dirt of the yard in front of the cabins and listened. The false dawn had paled the east. A truck made a thin insect whine in the distance, coming closer. He stood and listened to it. It went by at last, trailing a long sonorous unending burp. Frazier ran his hands through his hair and shuddered.

He took the restaurant key out of his pocket. It felt cool in his hand. Aside from himself and the girl, there were two other customers in the cabins. Their cabins were dark. A man snored heavily.

Frazier, keeping to the darkest shadows, moved soundlessly to the rear door of the restaurant. Getting each little bit of information from her had been like trying to pick up needles with his bare toes.

"I'd think a place like this would get knocked off."

"Knocked off?"

"Held up. You know. Robbers."

"Geez, honey, it's such a crummy little place."

"Well, that's the kind they pick. You know. Crazy kids."

"Honey, let's sleep for a while. Come on, Stan. Let's take a nap, huh?"

"Well, I'll tell you, if I owned it, I'd have some pro-tection."

"Aren't you sleepy a bit, hon? You could take a nap, but you'd have to be out of here before it's light."

"I'm not sleepy," he snarled.

"Well, you don't have to get snotty about it." She yawned. "I shouldn't have ought to let you come in here anyhow."

"I guess I just feel like talking. I didn't mean to get nasty."

She put her arm around him, patted his shoulder. "That's okay, darlin'. I'll talk if you want to talk. What should we talk about?"

"I was wondering if your boss ever got held up."

"Oh, him! He'd fight for his life to save a dime. He keeps some kind of gun in the drawer under the cash register."

"Take it home with him?"

"I don't think so."

He filed that fact away. It glowed in his mind. Her hand crept across his bare chest. He lay on his back with his hands behind his head. She giggled and said, "Daddy, you should have let me sleep some. Now I'm getting all gay again."

He forced himself to turn toward her and enfold her in his arms. Her body was moistly hot and her hair smelled of short order grease.

Later he asked, casually, "On account of you live right here and he lives down the road, do you open up in the morning?"

"Wha?"

He shook her soft shoulder. "Hey, do you have to open up in the morning?"

"Up till now. Not tomorrow, hon. Remember? I never open up this crummy joint again."

"You'll have to give him back his key."

"Wha?"

"His key, damn it. Where's his key?"

"Gee, beer makes me sleepy. It's in my purse."

He waited in the cabin, beside her, until the sound of her heavy breathing began to fill the enclosed space. He looked at her. Pale moonlight shone on a shadowed eye, a breast as white and heavy as lard. When he was certain her sleep was deep, he sat up and found his shoes, stood up and put on his clothing. He took her purse over to the window and found the key. The spring on the screen door tingled as he opened the door. He waited, listening to her breathing.

He tried the key in the back door of the restaurant. It turned easily in the lock. He went inside. The kitchen was small and it smelled bad, smelled of water-damp boards that rotted under linoleum, smelled of food scraps that decayed in out-of-the-way corners, smelled of the cold acid suds of the dishwater. A partition divided the kitchen from the eating area. There was a single swinging door with a round porthole in it. The dim glow of the night light came through the portal, making an orange highlight on the square white corner of the old refrigerator. Frazier pressed his fingertips against the door, opened it a crack and listened for traffic. The highway was silent. He moved into the restaurant proper, moved along behind the counter. The night light was a single orange bulb over the cash register. A refrigeration compressor started in the kitchen, startling him for a moment.

Frazier felt alert and alive. His fingertips tingled. His body felt hard and quick. His breathing was shallow with excitement. He moved closer to the cash register. He heard the hard onrushing song of a fast car. He crouched behind the counter, fingertips against the worn duckboards. The car hammered a fast hole through the night, dragging small whirlwinds behind it. Frazier stood up and found the drawer under the cash register. It was a wooden drawer, shallow, locked. He felt the underside of the drawer, felt the give of quarter-inch plywood. He knelt, listened to the silence, drove his fist up against the underside of the drawer. The wood splintered. He listened to the silence again. Two more cars went by. He got his fingertips in the split and gently pulled the wood apart. A gun in a leather holster slid down into his hand. He pulled the gap wider, reached in and felt a small box. He knew by the feel that it was ammunition. He removed the box, took the gun from the holster, slid the holster back up into the drawer and pressed the splintered bottom back into place.

The gun was a stubby, short-barreled revolver. He felt the barrel opening with his finger. He decided it was a .38, a better gun than he had planned on. He had expected a .32 automatic. He stood up and put the weapon in one side pocket of his trousers, the box of ammunition in the other. He had to duck once more as a truck labored by, heading toward the dawn. He went back through the kitchen, let himself out and locked the door. He took the key back to the girl's cabin. He put it in her purse. When he pushed the door open the spring made that noisy sound again.

"Whozzat?"

"Stan, honey. I'm going back to my place. It's nearly light."

"Oh. We really going today, darlin'?"

"Sure thing."

"Mmmm. That's good. That's awful good."

He heard her contented breathing. He went back to his own place, shut himself in the tiny primitive bathroom and looked the gun over. It was a Colt Detective Special, battered, ugly, ancient and deadly. He sighted it. It fit his hand well. The cylinder was fully loaded, the hammer resting on a live round. There were nineteen rounds in the box. He dropped the rounds, loose, into his left jacket pocket, tore the cardboard box to small pieces and flushed them down the toilet.

He took off his clothes, piled them in the corner, the weapon on top, and stepped into the cheap tin shower. The girl had made him feel soiled.

She had gotten off work at eleven. They had sat on the steps of her cabin, her cabin lights out, with the two six-packs of beer and the opener.

He had talked about the trip as a business proposition. "I've got a few hundred bucks. I can get Miranda out of hock and we can drive out there together. You say this Joey has a job lined up for you. Okay. So we keep track of what the trip costs and you pay me back out of what you earn out there. It's like a loan."

Her reluctance was only token. She clinked her can of beer against his and said, "Stan, we're in business. I can't wait to see his face when I tell him I'm through."

"Let's figure on getting out of here tomorrow morning, Donna."

"So why not? I can pack in ten minutes."

"It's a deal."

"Las Vegas, here we come."

He had leaned back with his elbow against the door sill. He ran the backs of his fingers up and down her bare arm. She giggled and moved away and said, "Remember? A business deal, Stan."

He had persisted. It had taken all of ten minutes before he had his arms around her, lips on hers, and she was drawing great shuddering breaths. And perhaps another twenty minutes before they had fumbled their way into the dark cabin, groping at each other, falling onto the lumpy bed.

In the act of love he felt apart from her, hovering over her, high, cruel, cold and remote, despising her and what happened to his body. It had ever been that way with women. It seemed, always, a defilement of his "apartness," a compromise of his cold need to walk alone. He looked down upon her induced anguish with contempt, feeling that his own response was weakness. Yet this was a thing to be done, a thing to bind her to him in stupid unquestioning faith and loyalty, because her greatest use would come if he could make her believe, without question, that black was white and up was down.

Now he scrubbed his body vigorously, and turned the water cold to rinse away the suds. He dried himself, picked up the gun, turned out the light and found his bed in the darkness.

He wedged the gun between springs and mattress. He thought about killing her. Maybe she would be the one. The others had been legal, authorized. He thought of how it would be. Take a back road into the hills. He'd aim at her belly and watch her face when he pulled the trigger. He smiled at the dark ceiling.

The dream wrenched Jamison awake. The blue car was rolling like a tarpon and he was flying through the air. . . . He came awake trembling, his pajamas dank with cold sweat. He got up and went into the bathroom, took the pajamas off in the darkness and toweled his trembling body. It took a long time for his heart to slow down. He turned on the lights to find fresh pajamas. Later he sat in darkness on the edge of the bed, arms braced on his knees, cigarette glowing.

He thought of Kathryn Aller. Her room would be dark. No, there would probably be a night light. The pale glow of it would be against her still face. The mind, deep in blackness, would not know of the room or the light. Beneath the stillness of her face the mind struggled for its survival, struggled to heal its hurts. The body, uninjured, rested and waited for command. Heart pulsed, organs performed their blind functions, glands secreted, muscles lay slack and waited. Deep in the mind all the bright memories would wait, unused, like cards in a drawer.

Deep in the earth all of Gina's memories were cards in a drawer that was locked forever. All of her was stilled.

At last he knew he could sleep again.

Joyce Conklin was awakened by the sounds Paul was making in his sleep. They had both fallen asleep in her bed. He made thin whinnying sounds in his throat that would have been ludicrous had they not been so indicative of fright. His legs twitched as though, in his lost dream, he ran in endless terror.

She put her hand against his cheek. "It's all right, darling. Everything is all right."

He tried to start up, but she pressed him gently back. "You're safe, dear. Everything is all right."

He seemed to stop breathing for a moment, gave a long trembling sigh and turned on his other side, pinning her arm. His breathing quieted and he nestled down into sleep. She smiled at his back and whispered once more, "Yes, everything is all right."

She felt an infinite tenderness toward this strange and complicated human being who was, so miraculously, her husband. She had sensed his torments, understood intuitively the way he had tried to hurt himself—and her. Now, strangely, he had been brought back to her out of the dark places of his soul. She was deeply grateful for that.

Yet, watching him in the darkness, she knew in her heart that this would not last. He might be back with her for a year, or two, or three. Then again his malformed emotions would drive him into new areas of pain. For now she would let him believe that she believed that this regained closeness would be permanent. She would make as much of it as she could, as though storing away warmth against the inevitable winter. He would go away again and, with luck, would come back another time.

This, then, was her destiny, her cyclical love. She knew she would not trade it. She knew it was what she wanted. Let others have the placid plateaus of uneventful contentment. Her love might descend often into pain and darkness, but when it arose again into the light, it reached higher and farther than others could know.

She touched her lips lightly to his sleeping back, then gingerly wormed her arm out from under him. She slipped out of the bed and covered him over, giving the blanket little pats.

She stood slim and nude in the darkness between the beds, looking down at the darkness that was his head on the pillow. Night breeze from the open window made a coolness around her flanks. She slipped into his bed, curling and hugging herself for the warmth that came quickly. She lay with her eyes wide open, watching him as he slept.

The ache of hand and wrist brought Suzie reluctantly up out of her dreams. She had been sitting in Barney's Merc with Devlin Jamison. It was night and Barney stood out by the hood of the Merc, ruining it. He kept tearing strips off the hood, just like it was tinfoil, and Mr. Jamison had his arm around her and they were both laughing at Barney.

Every time she awakened there was the same little shock of realizing where she was and remembering what had happened. This time it was a little different because she wanted her mother. She felt lonesome in the night and she wanted her mother dreadfully. Just the touch of her. Just to know she was there. Suzie cried a little. She did not cry long. She reached for a Kleenex on the night stand and blew her nose heartily.

She thought of the second visit from Devlin Jamison and the second visit from Uncle Bernie. She wished she knew what they had said to each other. They certainly had it all figured out. Just what she would do practically every single minute for the next five years. It had sounded like an awful stupid way to spend your life—going to school.

But Devlin—she felt a warm tingling when she thought of him by his first name—had looked at her so solemnly and said, "I want you to promise, Susan, that you'll do your very best."

Like a dope she had promised. Then Uncle Bernie had confirmed what was going to happen and said that Devlin was paying for it. It seemed such a darn pointless thing when. . . .

She suddenly held her breath and stared wide-eyed at the shadow pattern of the night light. Gosh, that could be it! What would an important man like Mr. Jamison want with a seventeen-year-old high school kid? But if he took that same kid and waited for five years, waited until she had every advantage and could be a good hostess, and companion and . . . wife.

Brother! Sure, that was why he'd been so insistent and made her promise. He couldn't tell her why, because he was afraid it would hurt her feelings.

Her cheeks felt hot and a good warmth suffused her. She closed her eyes and, moving her lips, made a solemn promise. "Devlin, I promise that I will do just what you want me to do. I'll study hard and learn all the right things to do. I'll learn how to talk the way you do, and try to have good taste, and I'll never do anything like with Barney, and after five years I'll be just what you want me to be." She tried to think of a suitable seal to finish off the promise, and then whispered, "So help me God." She bit her lip and, after a while added, "And I'll get slimmer in the hips."

The man sat in the dark third-floor office on a chair pulled close to the open window. His forearm rested on the window sill, and his chin was on his wrist. He could see down into the fenced rear yard of the Ace Garage. The street light shone on the cars in the rear yard, over a dozen of them. The man could see the ruined Cadillac, the gutted Olds. He put the night glasses to his eyes and the rear of the Olds looked close enough to touch. He could see where the streetlight touched a narrow segment of the two tires in the rear luggage compartment. He put the glasses down on the sill and yawned, scrubbed at his eyes. It was a hell of a long night. There had been lots of long nights and there would be many more to come. Years of them. Funny damn way to use a law degree, he thought.

chapter 17

AT eight o'clock Frazier walked over to her cabin and peered in at her through the screen. She lay on her stomach with her face in the pillow, snoring, the blanket down around her waist.

He called her name three times and she didn't answer. He went in and shook her awake. She rolled over and covered herself up and promised she'd get right up. He went back to his cabin.

The owner arrived at eight-thirty. Frazier watched him head toward Donna's cabin, jaw outthrust, face red. He heard them yelling at each other. He could not hear what was said. The man went lunging back to the restaurant, unlocked the rear door, banged it back against the side of the building and went in.

At nine-fifteen Frazier went over again. She was asleep. He went in and grabbed her wrists and pulled her to a sitting position. She looked at him with dulled eyes. At last he got her awake. "Come on! Come on! We got to get on the road, sugar."

She yawned. "Okay, okay. Say, he was in here, yammering at me. I told him I quit."

"I know. And then you went back to sleep. Get up, damn you."

She pouted. "You don't want to talk to me like that."

"Pretty please. Get up. Just for me."

"You get out and I'll get dressed."

When he went over at quarter of ten she was in a bathrobe, washing things in the small bathroom sink. "Aren't you ready yet?"

"It won't take long now. Honest. These things dry fast. They're nylon."

"Are you packed?"

"That won't take only a couple of minutes. We don't have to make any special place by tonight, do we?"

"I'm itchy to get on the road."

147

"I hate having you see me with my hair like this. I'll come over when I'm ready. I'll hurry, honest."

It was five minutes of eleven when she came out of the cabin with a big dark blue suitcase and a bright red hatbox. She wore a pale gray sweater, dark blue slacks and sandals. She had a gray and white scarf tied around her hair. He had to admit to himself that she looked better than he had expected her to look.

She looked at him shyly. "I guess I finally made it, Stan."

"I guess you did. Here. I'll take the suitcase."

"Are we going to phone for a cab?"

"It's only a half-mile."

The owner came to the doorway of the restaurant and stood with his hands on his hips and watched them as they walked by the front door. As soon as they were by he spat and turned and went back inside. Cars whistled by them, kicking up dust from the shoulder.

"I bet you think I'm terrible," she said.

"How so?"

"Last night. I was cheap to let you do that." She looked appealingly up at him as they walked side by side. He noted that there were tiny beads of effort on her round face.

"I don't think that at all." He searched for the words. "Donna, I think it was just the way it should have been. Just the way it had to be, with us."

She sighed and shifted the hatbox to her other hand. It thumped annoyingly against his leg. "Ooops. Sorry. Gee, Stan, I'm so glad you feel that way, honest. I was afraid of what you might think of me."

"Skip it, sugar." He lengthened his stride.

"Gee, you got long legs, darlin'."

He looked ahead. He could see the sign above the building. A red neon diamond with the word "Ace" spelled out inside the diamond.

Jamison was sitting beside Kathryn Aller's bed at nine o'clock when Dilby came in to look at the patient.

"Here again, I see!" Dilby said in his exuberant voice.

Jamison got up. "Good morning, Doctor. The nurse told me she had her eyes open earlier this morning."

"Well! Let's see here." Dilby fussed over the patient. He finally spoke her name loudly in her ear, slapping her cheek lightly with his finger tips. "Kathryn! Kathy! Wake up!" He turned and said to Jamison, "If you can find the right nick-name, they respond better."

Kathryn Aller opened her unswollen eye. Jamison moved closer to the bed. The color was not precisely blue, nor was it pure gray. The expression in her eye was dreadfully blank. It did not focus on anything. It was merely open.

"That's a good girl," Dilby said jovially. "Fine girl! Now let's see you raise your arm. This one. The right one." He touched her hand. She raised her arm. "Put it down, dear. That's a good bright girl! Now the other one. Splendid. Nurse, get me a glass of water." The nurse brought the water. Dilby got his arm under the patient, raised her up and held the glass to her lips. "Let's see if you can drink this, Kath-ryn." He tilted the glass and the girl swallowed obediently until it was empty. Dilby lowered her back and she lay with her head on the pillow, looking blankly at the ceiling.

Dilby smiled affectionately at Jamison. "Coming along. She'll do what you tell her to do now. Nurse, I think you can get her to eat normally now. We want to keep those muscles in tone. This afternoon get her into a robe and make her walk up and down the corridor."

Jamison said awkwardly, "Could . . . would it be all right if I did that? I mean the nurse could get her into a robe. I'd be glad to walk her."

Dilby said, "We'll take all the help we can get, won't we, nurse?"

Jamison looked at the girl. Her eye had closed again.

Dilby laughed and said, "Get in here at noon and we'll even let you feed her. She'll chew and swallow once the food is in her mouth, but somebody will have to order her to open her mouth each time and then poke the food in. Want to try that too, Mr. Jamison?"

"I might as well."

"We'll make you an honorary nurse's aid around here. One thing, though. The way she's reacting, she may come out of this zombie phase at any time, come back to complete aware-ness. When she does she may have a violent emotional reac-tion. Do what you can to comfort her, and get word to me."

After Dilby left, Jamison went outside. It was a fine morn-ing, clear and warm, with a cloudless sky. He decided to walk down to town. He could look in at the garage. He wanted to see how the car looked. That would be a sufficient excuse. He remembered how delighted Gina had been when they had gone down and picked up that car. She had loved convertibles, loved wind in her hair. Her driving had always been more exuberant than accurate.

"The thing I like best," she had said solemnly, "is the way the new ones smell."

"You know, Gina, in the used car lots when they get a good clean car in, a recent model, they sometimes brush the upholstery with embalming fluid. That gives it a new car smell. Psychological salesmanship."

"How dreadful!" she had said. "How perfectly awful!"

Gina's sense of humor had always failed abruptly when the humor became the least bit macabre. She had had an almost pathological fear of death, of anything concerning death. Death to her was as darkness to a timid child. It was full of unknown horrors. And he had had to let the child walk off, alone, into the darkness, powerless to hold her back.

His thoughts had dimmed the day. He wrested his mind away from thoughts of Gina, back to thoughts of Kathryn Aller. He passed a school and heard the thin sweet voices of a young class singing. He walked by his hotel and on down toward the south end of the town, toward the highway and the garage and the car in which, by all rights, he should have died. The rapid walking was stretching the lingering soreness and stiffness out of his muscles. Wednesday. The accident seemed a month ago. Not just two days ago. Incredible that it should be only two days ago.

After a long, late, lazy breakfast Joyce smiled across the table at Paul and said, "What now, sire? Watch the changing of the guard? Float about on the canals?"

"This is like a weird sea voyage," Paul said. "No responsibility. Nothing at all to do. Want to phone the kids again?"

"Later. Let's see. I'd like to take a long walk on a back road. Then come back famished and have lunch. Then go to a cowboy movie. Then phone the kids."

"Program approved. Let's start our walk by the garage. I want to stop in and see how they're coming."

Frazier and Donna walked into the garage. They stopped by the small high desk. Frazier felt the stiffness of tension in his shoulders. The garage was busy. Tools clanged on concrete. A motor raced. The air was blued with exhaust stink.

The service manager came over and Donna said, "Hey there. Remember me? I've come to bail out Miranda."

"Sure. How you doing? The cashier will have the final bill, miss. Right over there. Going to take off?"

"Think she'll get us to Las Vegas?"

"There and back, if you want to come back."

Donna laughed. "No thanks."

"The car is out in back."

Frazier said, "Is it okay with you if I check it over some before we take off?"

The service manager shrugged. "Go ahead."

They went to the cashier's window and Frazier paid the bill. The girl stamped the receipt and passed it out to him with his change and the car keys. They carried the suitcase and hatbox back through the garage and out into the wire-fenced yard. Donna walked directly over to an elderly tan Studebaker and patted the front fender.

"Here she is! Pretty jaunty, hey?"

He loaded the suitcase and hatbox into the rear seat. He walked around it, inspecting the tires. He got in and started the motor. He raced it. It sounded all right to him. He left it idling and got out, scratched his head.

"What's the matter, honey?"

"Sounds a little ragged. I better check it over." He opened the hood and started in at the motor. "I can make some adjustments, Donna." He took a five-dollar bill out of his wallet and handed it to her. "Why don't you roam around and buy yourself something? This'll take me a half-hour or so. Wait for me at that drugstore across the way."

"Well . . . okay. Thanks. Don't get all dirty, Stan."

She walked back into the garage, glancing back once, smiling and giving him a wave of her hand. Frazier looked in the back end and found a ratty-looking screwdriver. He noticed that the spare was badly worn. He left the back end open. He went around and leaned across the front fender and reached into the mysterious motor with the screwdriver, careful not to touch anything.

A mechanic parked a car in the back yard and walked back into the garage. Frazier, looking back over his shoulder, could see the Olds, see the edge of the two tires. The gun in the right pocket of the cheap jacket bumped against the fender of the Studebaker. He rehearsed his movements. Walk quickly and calmly over, hoist the lid, pull out the tire, lug it back and sling it into the rear compartment of the Studebaker, bang the lid shut.

A tall well-dressed man with a bandaged face walked out

into the rear yard with the service manager and walked over to the Cad. They stood and looked at it and talked. Frazier cursed them silently. The service manager went back inside. The tall man stood there, just staring, as if he had fallen asleep on his feet. Frazier seethed with impatience. To make matters worse a young couple came out and walked over to the Cadillac. They started to talk to the tall man. They all shook hands. The idling motor of the Studebaker began to generate considerable heat. He looked at the three people. Hell, it was obvious they weren't with the garage. Maybe they had been in the same accident, or seen it or something. Or maybe the tall man was the insurance man, or the smaller man.

If you did a thing calmly, as if it was your business, people generally accepted it. He had a habit that had been with him a long time. He counted to ten. At the count of ten he turned and walked briskly, though not too fast, over to the burned Olds. He took hold of the trunk compartment and lifted it up and grasped the tire. It came out easily, rim and all. Too easily. He remembered it as being heavier.

There was a great whuffing sound he could not identify. And a great brass voice filled the world, saying, "Frazier, drop the tire and lay face down on the ground. You're surrounded, Frazier. Give up!"

The man in the high window had been grievously startled. He had seen the man in the yellow leather jacket and the plump girl in blue and gray come out and put luggage in an old car. He had watched them through the glasses for a few moments and then relaxed. The girl had gone away and the man fiddled with the car. A tall man and the service manager came out and looked at the Cadillac. The tall man was alone there for a time and then a couple joined him.

The man in the window yawned. The sun was hot. The yawn squinched his eyes shut. When he opened them the man in the yellow leather jacket was halfway to the Olds. He watched almost stupidly while the man yanked the telltale tire out. He clicked the ready switch and said to the cars, "Come on in. On the double. He's in the yard." He pulled the other hand mike over, clicked it on, waited a moment and then blew into it. The speaker on the post in the corner of the yard whuffed. He gave his orders to Frazier and picked the rifle up, worked the bolt, put the stock against his shoulder and looked down through the scope, centering the cross hairs on Frazier's chest.

Frazier darted to the left, out of the field of the scope. The man swung the scope over and saw that Frazier had a gun in his hand, had grabbed the slim pretty girl who had been standing by the Cadillac and swung her in front of him, an arm around her waist. The two men with the girl stared. The smaller one started forward and the bigger one grabbed him, pulled him back.

Frazier was looking wildly around in all directions. He pulled the girl toward the Studebaker. The man in the window saw one of the cars alerted by the radio swing in toward the front of the garage, out of sight, stopping to block the exit.

Frazier shoved the girl into the car and got in behind her. The man in the window saw that the girl would be over behind the wheel, with Frazier holding the gun on her. He wondered if he should try the microphone again. The car began to move forward. It turned and the man in the window could see Frazier's right elbow. It rested on the window sill of the car, sharply bent, as he held the gun on the girl.

The man in the window made his decision. He had previously adjusted the scope for firing down from an angle. He centered the cross hairs on the exposed elbow, moving the rifle with the movement of the car, squeezing the trigger off gently. He prayed that the jar would not yank Frazier's trigger finger.

Through the scope he saw the elbow leap and smash, deformed with impact. The other door opened and the girl tumbled out onto her hands and knees. The car kept going and hit the side of the building near the doorway into the garage. The girl got up and the smaller of the two men ran to her, held her in his arms. The big man ran to the car, yanked the door open, hauled Frazier out, shook him, threw him aside, reached into the car and brought the gun out. Men came running.

Soon the man in the window could no longer see Frazier. He stood the rifle in a corner, took out his handkerchief and wiped the palms of his hands. When he looked down again he saw the girl in gray and blue struggling to get through the crowd around Frazier. He leaned close to the live mike and said, "Grab that girl there in gray sweater, blue slacks. She was with him."

chapter 18

On Thursday, May twenty-eighth, Jamison walked Kathryn Aller around the hospital grounds for the tenth consecutive day. The bandage on her head was much smaller. Her dark blonde hair was neatly brushed. There were a few greenish and yellowish traces of the great bruise which had puffed and darkened her face. She wore a gray tailored suit, a white blouse, crepe-soled moccasins.

"Once around again?" he asked, and heard the sound of his own voice and realized how much he sounded like Dilby. Bluff professional cheer. The girl did not answer. He liked the way she walked. Tall, composed, with slender grace. She handled herself well, even though she was unconscious of it. She could follow the simplest orders, yet once they were completed she would remain frozen, in stasis, unable to go further. Given simple food and told to eat, and with the fork placed in her hand, she would feed herself. Given meat, knife and fork, she was helpless. When she walked she avoided simple obstructions.

He took her arm and gently guided her toward the bench. "Now we'll sit for a while and talk, shall we?"

At the bench he took her shoulders, turned her around and said, "Sit down, Kathryn." She sat on the bench and he sat beside her.

Dr. Dilby called it an impairment of consciousness, traumatic. He said that sometimes, rarely, it could be caused by emotional shock. He said he wondered if there wasn't some of that involved in this case, along with the actual physical injury. Dilby said to try to stimulate her into talking, into accepting increasing responsibility for herself.

"Can you say hello, Kathryn? Try. Say hello. Hello."

She licked her lips. Her throat worked. "Hello." Though her voice was low, and of pleasant timbre, there was absolutely no expression in her tone. It was as flat as the "mama" of a doll.

"Look at me, Kathryn. Here." He touched her chin,

154

turned her face toward him gingerly. She looked at him and through him.

"Can you say my name? Dev. Dev. Say it. Dev."

"Dev."

"That's the way, Kathryn. Now what will we talk about? Would you like to hear a letter I got today? It's from that girl who was here, the one who was hurt the same time you were. I've got it right here. Here we go.

"'Dear Mr. Jamison. They are nice to me here. They say my leg won't have to be bandaged much longer. I can do lots more things for myself. It isn't so hard using just one arm when you get used to it. The papers from the camp came today. There are pictures. I didn't know Maine looked like that. There is a list of what I have to have. I have nearly everything except a riding habit. I thought at first that was like a smoking habit. Ha ha. They sail too. Did you know that?

"'I will be glad to go there because nearly all the people here are old. A boy I knew drove way over here to see me, five hundred miles. He brought candy but I gave it away because I am not eating sweet things any more. He stayed two hours and he bored me. He's young and acts silly. He used to be one of my best friends. I have told them here that you will come and see me here before I go to camp in July. Will you?

"'You said I should ask for what I need. For the measurements for my riding pants, I am five feet five, and twenty-three inches around the middle and thirty-two inches around the fanny, but by the time I will need them for riding on a horse for the first time, I will be maybe only thirty around. The X-rays of my arm and hand were good, they say. If you could send me a picture of you I would like it very much. Very sincerely yours, Susan.'

"Isn't that a nice letter? When she gets out of that convalescent home, she's going to go away to summer camp. Then in the fall she's going to a private school in Baltimore, where my wife went when she was young."

Kathryn Aller stared straight ahead. Sometimes it made him feel like a fool, talking to her when there was absolutely no response.

Sometimes, looking at her still face, her quiet mouth, he wondered what a kiss would do to her. It was standard procedure for princesses, sleeping variety. It made him feel both excited and guilty to think of that. It seemed an extension of the dreams of small boys.

"Kathryn, you are a lovely woman," he said. He sighed, put his hand on hers. "Well, come on, old girl. Time to walk you back inside." He stood up and looked down at her. "Stand up, Kathryn."

She did not move. He frowned. That was a simple order she had obeyed readily before. "Stand up, Kathryn!"

She did not move. He looked at her closely. Her lips were moving. Her eyes had narrowed a bit. She was looking beyond the far trees, and for the first time her eyes seemed to have focus. He sat down suddenly beside her and took her cool hand.

"Kathryn! Are you waking up? Are you waking up, dear?"

She looked down at his hands on hers and then looked sharply, quickly into his face. Her eyes were alert, alive, frightened. She yanked her hand away, pushed back away from him, sliding along the bench and stood up.

"Who are you?" she asked, her voice thin with alarm.

He got up and she backed away from him. He took two running steps and caught her wrists, held her strongly. She struggled. "Let go! Where am I? What is going on?"

"Kathryn. Please. Listen to me."

"Let go of me. Let—go!"

"I can't. You have to listen. Kathryn, listen to me. Today is the twenty-eighth of May."

She struggled on for a few seconds and then stopped struggling and stared at him. "It's the seventeenth!"

"No, it isn't. You've been sick. You were hurt. In an accident."

She frowned. "Was Walter . . ." She shook her head as though trying to clear it. "No. I was . . . I was. . . . The car spun around and . . ."

She put her chin down against her chest and began to cry. He held her wrists helplessly. He released her wrists. She took a wavering sideways step and then moved forward, leaned against him. He held her, his arms around her. Her long body trembled and she made stifled sounds. After a while he gave her his handkerchief, guided her to the bench. She sat down heavily, wearily.

With the handkerchief against her eyes she said, "My head aches. I'm so awfully tired."

"These are hospital grounds. We can go back in and you can go to bed."

"I'd like that. Have I been . . . wild? Raving or anything?"

"No. You've been half-asleep."

"Are you my doctor?"

"No. I . . . I was in the same accident."

"Did a Mr. Walter Houde come to see me?"

"No. No one came."

"I'm so tired."

"Come on then. We'll go back in."

She leaned on him heavily. He took her to her room. She started to unbutton her suit jacket. He closed the door and went off to find Dr. Dilby. He felt like singing. She had come willingly into his arms to cry. She would need him. Her need of him filled his emptiness. He had had his first glimpse of her, of what she was, and he liked what he saw. He burst in on Dilby. Dilby, using a rubber hammer on a fat woman's knee, glared at him.

On that same day, May twenty-eighth, Roger Seiver mailed the letter to Mrs. Stanley Cherrik. It had been prepared with the utmost care, and he mailed it reluctantly. It might cost Jamison a pretty penny before it was all over, but the fool had been adamant—and it was his money.

Seiver knew the opening of the letter by heart.

My dear Mrs. Cherrik:

A man who prefers to remain anonymous and who was impressed by the selfless heroism displayed by your late husband in the accident that caused his death, has asked me to act as intermediary in a plan which he sincerely hopes you will accept. My client wishes to set up a fund which will provide . . ."

And, on May twenty-eighth, at three fifty-one P.M., eleven miles east of Blanchard, a young girl driving her father's Buick at an excessive rate of speed gravely misjudged the clearance available when she attempted to pass, in the center lane, between a car in the left lane and a truck in the right. A light rain spoiled traction and the back end of the Buick swung as she realized her error and applied her brakes.

And the burst and smash of multiple collision was like a deep cough in a metal chest. Glass sprayed in elfin angel noise on wet concrete. Oil dripped and reeked on hot over-turned metal. Tires screamed their panic chorus. And soon came the sirens, howling down under the wet sky. Soon came the wreckers and the white jackets and the arrogant whistles.

Clear the way. Come on. Get rolling, lady. Keep the line moving.

There's nothing to see.

She was very young.

She was dangerous.

She was a girl who lived too close
     to the edge of violence.

She hunted trouble.

She was an exhibitionist,
     a body worshipper, a sensualist.

She was without morals, scruples, ethics.

She was totally, utterly beautiful.

She was . . .

CLEMMIE

A violent and haunting novel
by bestselling author

JOHN D. MacDONALD

R 1733   60¢

A Fawcett Gold Medal Book

On sale wherever paperback books are available